The Traveler II

Jon Simpson and Mike Simpson

AuthorHouse™
1663 Liberty Drive
Bloomington, IN 47403
www.authorhouse.com
Phone: 1 (800) 839-8640

This book is printed on acid-free paper.

ISBN: 978-1-7283-4109-5 (sc)
ISBN: 978-1-7283-4110-1 (e)

Library of Congress Control Number: 2019921228

Print information available on the last page.

Published by AuthorHouse 01/03/2020

Contents

Part III

Opening Old Wounds

Chapter 1

"Sebastian," Ashleigh said frantically. "Did you see where it went!?" Sebastian swung his torch in an arc, trying to spot the creature. "I thought you saw where it went" he replied." Ashleigh glared at him, to which he simply smiled and turned his attention back to the task at hand. "Have you any idea what kind of demon we're dealing with yet?" Ashleigh pulled out the journal, gesturing for Sebastian to bring the torch towards her so she could read. In these past few months Ashleigh had gotten used to reading Sebastian's journal, learning where each chapter was and knowing the difference between one monster and the other. "It took me some time, but I've boiled it down to one particular demon." She skimmed the pages, searching for the right one. As she read, she felt Sebastian pull her away from her position as a rock flew past her, shattering against the nearby wall. "Careful, I'm not going to always be there to help you."

Ashleigh nodded in thanks, turning back to the book, trying to avoid any more incoming debris. "Can't you do something to calm it down so I can read? It's not easy to read with minimal lighting and an angry demon throwing stones at you." Sebastian dodged a rock, catching it in his hands. "No not really," he said. "Unless you can figure out what this thing is, I'm a bit incapacitated at the moment." Ashleigh rushed towards a wall with some light peering through, trying to use it to the best degree so she could see. "Almost there... Ah found it." Sebastian swatted a final rock away followed Ashleigh, hoping she found the answer they needed. I can't quite understand its name, but this fits with everything we heard on the way here. Causes mischief, possesses nearby objects, and so on. But I can't read its name. Amen... Omen... Can you possibly read it?"

Sebastian answered without even reading the book. "Aamon," Sebastian snatched the book, taking a closer look. "Are you sure? Are you positively sure?" Ashleigh leaned over his shoulder. "Yes," she said. "It's right here and everything fits." She looked up and saw Sebastian beaded with sweat, mumbling random sentences to himself. "That can't be possible, he was sealed away decades ago... unless someone let him out. But who could have... Suddenly, the temple began to rumble and shake, causing Ashleigh to stumble into the wall. Before she could fully steady herself, she felt Sebastian grab her arm and pull her towards the exit. "We need to leave, now." He grabbed Ashleigh's arm, pulling her back the way they came. "Why?" she said. "We can handle it, it's no different from the other creatures we faced so far, is it?" Sebastian didn't listen. He continued to pull Ashleigh through the long underground tunnel. "No, you don't understand. This thing. If it is Aamon..." Sebastian was interrupted by a low growl that grew behind them. Ashleigh looked back towards the direction they came from, wondering what could possibly worry Sebastian so much about this creature. "Sebastian," Ashleigh said, trying to calm him down. But before she could say anything else, a force pushed them against a wall, followed by a deep, threatening voice.

"You were very unwise to come here, fallen child," the voice said. It sounded like dull daggers scraping against stone. "To think someone such as yourself would attempt to breech my home." Ashleigh watched as a lantern lifted itself from a nearby sconce on the wall and floated towards Sebastian's face. It inched closer and closer until it was within inches, his face glowing orange from the light of the flame. "First off," Sebastian said, moving his face as far away from the flame as possible. "This isn't your home and you know it, but rather it is the temple of which The Son was born in, and to call it your temple is blasphemy upon itself. And second, we didn't even know you were you here, otherwise I would have never come here so unprepared." As he finished his sentence, a black silhouette appeared, revealing itself to be the force that was holding the torch. It looked like the Dybbuk that they had faced months ago, except this creature had more form; it was draped in black robes decorated with golden accents, and it had two curved horns protruding from its forehead. Its claws twitched as it held the torch "Hmmm,' Aamon mumbled. "You use words like those self-proclaimed 'crusaders of god'. But you appear to be much ruder than they are." He inched its face closer to Sebastian's, and Ashleigh could see it had eyes and no mouth, just like the Dybbuk. The only difference was that its eyes were not glowing red but were a sickly gold. Not like a fresh gold coin, but more like an old coin left in a spittoon for far too long. Ashleigh strained to move against the wall, but her body was pinned so she could face directly towards Sebastian and Aamon. "Let him go you faulty, gilded Dybbuk."

The demon turned directly towards her, giving her an intense glare. "My my, he said walking towards her. "Never before have I met such a simple woman with such tenacity. You think yourself better than I to compare me to such a lowly creature as the Dybbuk? I am the one who birthed that creature and I can birth things far worse than you could dare to comprehend." He lifted his other claw and lightly scratched her cheek, drawing a small amount of blood. "If I could I would show you my true form right now, introducing you to but a taste of the level of fear

I can instill in you." Sebastian turned his head to face Ashleigh, trying to warn her not to continue, but he was too late to stop her. "Well to tell you the truth," she began. "I've faced death against a sexist Strigoi, nearly had a heart attack or two when facing the Dybbuk, and I even managed to get you upset by an insult from, how did you put it? 'A simple woman?'" She turned her head to face directly towards the Demon, glaring into its old gold eyes. "I personally feel like I have dealt with some fairly intense ordeals, especially the Dybbuk. So to me, insulting you is a bit of a bonus." Ashleigh looked out the corner of her eye at Sebastian, only to see that he was looking at her with wide eyes, almost as if he just watched her make the biggest mistake of her life.

Aamon stared at her for another moment, his claw itching next to her cheek. And then, he began laughing. It started small, but grew into almost an excited child's laughter. He looked over at Sebastian smiling, or at the very least his cheeks were raised in such a way it looked like a smile. "Who would have guessed that people like you could ever find someone with such courage," he bellowed. He looked back at Ashleigh, removing his claw. "I am impressed by your courage young girl, and for that I won't make you or your friend suffer. But if either of you return here again," he looked between her and Sebastian, and then back at her with squinted eyes. "I will not be so kind." After his last words he placed his hand over Ashleigh's face, and all she saw was darkness.

When Ashleigh came to, she sat upright as fast as possible, only to be caught off guard by the glaring sunlight. As her eyes adjusted, she placed her hands on her face, feeling the bloody scratch that Aamon had made. She took in her surroundings and saw that she and Sebastian were now miles away from the city. She couldn't help but notice how beautiful of a view it was, seeing the city of Nazareth from so far away. But before she could admire the view any further, her thoughts were interrupted by the sound of Sebastian groaning. She looked to around one more time and realized that she had somehow missed Sebastian lying on his stomach in the hot sun. She rushed to his side, turning him over. "Sebastian," she said shaking his shoulders. "Are you alright?" He suddenly shot upright and spat out a large amount of sand. She patted his back as he continued to cough for another minute. "I'm fine," he mumbled while wiping his face. "But Ashleigh, what you did back there..." Ashleigh cut him short before he could finish. "I know I'm sorry I was stupid and I panicked. I was caught up in the moment and he just looked so much like the Dybbuk we faced and I was terrified of what he might do to you and..." Sebastian lightly smacked her on the head, stopping her from talking any further. "First, calm down. And second, yes you were stupid." Ashleigh dropped her head, looking at the ground. She sat there quiet till she felt Sebastian's hand rub her head gently. She looked up at him confused and saw that he was smiling. "But, if you hadn't gotten his attention like you did, we might be dead right now." She smiled back at him, sitting next to him on the hot sand. "I'm still sorry though," she said. He looked over at her, placing his arm around her shoulder as comfort. "Its fine Ashleigh, I understand. And... I'm sorry too." She turned her head to face him, seeing that his attention had been redirected towards the city. "It's just that I should've seen this for what it was. I knew it was too coincidental that people were claiming there was such a terrible presence here, even with all the minor attacks." He stared off at the city once more, his hands shaking. Ashleigh placed her hand on his, trying to calm him down. "Sebastian," she said. "What is Aamon?" Sebastian looked at the ground, trying to find the courage to talk about what he knew.

"Aamon is... a very powerful demon. He is what is referred to as a 'Grand Marquis of Hell'. He controls forty infernal legions and is a demon of Goetia. He's very powerful and very dangerous, and was supposed to have been sealed away decades ago by a group of powerful priests." He looked back down at the ground, clenching his fists. "Those damn fools... They didn't do what they should've done." Ashleigh grew concerned, having not seen Sebastian get this worked up. "Well can't we go talk to these priests?" she asked. "Maybe that can help seal him away again. Sebastian turned to face her, a look of dread filling his eyes. "The thing is," he began. "When they sealed him away the first time, there were four priests. Three of them died and the only one left alive is..." he couldn't finish the statement. "He... what? What about him Sebastian?"

He chose not to finish the statement. "The point is, we can't go to them for help. We'll come back another time." Sebastian stood up and dusted the sand off his coat. There are others more capable of handling this..."Oh no you don't," Ashleigh yelled, standing up and stopping Sebastian from doing anything else. "We are not leaving this alone just because you have cold feet. You didn't abandon those people in Scotland when they needed you, even when you had the chance to. We didn't abandon the people in that village who were being tortured by Aamon, despite their warnings and discouragement. And you most certainly didn't abandon my home when women were getting killed by that pig of a Vampire. So to hear you say that 'there are other people who can take care of this' is the biggest load of horse shit I've heard in a long time. And that's saying something considering I grew up in a bar where people will make any excuse to get out of paying their tab." Sebastian turned away from Ashleigh. "Ashleigh you don't understand…" He was interrupted by Ashleigh grabbing his face and making him look at her. "No Sebastian, you don't understand. I came with you for a reason. You aren't the type to just give up at the drop of a pin when something gets tuff. Whatever reason you have for not wanting to talk about this priest, that's all and good I will not force you to tell me. But I will not let you give up on these people, on me, and most importantly." She placed her other hand on his face, looking him directly in the eyes. "You are not giving up on yourself."

Sebastian was awestruck at how intense she could be. He wondered how she could be this head strong until he realized she began to have tears in her eyes, as well as her hands were shaking as she held him. She was terrified for him and genuinely cared for his safety. He slowly grabbed her hands, pulling them down from his face. They were cold with adrenaline and shook worse than if they were frostbitten. "You know, you surprise me every day Ashleigh Briner." Her face eased up, and she buried her eyes into his sand covered coat. He patted her head, comforting her as she began to cry in his chest. As he held her he suddenly felt a fist in his stomach, forcing him to cough. "What was that for?" he said while laughing and coughing. "For making me cry in the scorching desert you twat," she mumbled in the ruffles of his coat. "Fair enough," he said. He looked down at Ashleigh, and then back at the city. "If you're as set in stone with helping these people as I think you are," he began. "Then I'm sure I can handle one priest for a day." Ashleigh looked up at him, her face red and covered in both sweat and tears. "What changed your mind so suddenly?" she asked. "Oh you know. Stubborn Irish temper, same as usual I suppose." Ashleigh prepared to punch him again, only to replace it with a hug. "There's the Sebastian I know," she said happily. Sebastian smiled down at her, only for his grin to be replaced by a look of unease.

"I just hope they don't shoot me on sight when we arrive." "I beg your pardon?" Ashleigh asked. "What do you mean, 'shoot you on sight?'" Sebastian forced a laugh. "Oh it's nothing to worry about yet. Now, let's return to the city to see if we can't get some supplies to make it to Haifa. If we want to find this priest we need to get on our way as soon as possible." Ashleigh hurried up to follow Sebastian, trying to maintain her balance in the sand. It wasn't easy trying to maintain footing in the every changing dunes when all you're wearing was simple walking boots. "Ok first," she began. What do you mean it's nothing to worry about yet? You just said you hope they don't shoot you on sight, and I can't decide whether you were joking or being serious. And second, where exactly are we going? You never did say who or where this priest is." Sebastian continued walking, turning back only for a second to look at Ashleigh. "Well to answer your first question, it really is nothing to worry about. As long as we don't end up at gun point when we arrive." Ashleigh grumbled, causing Sebastian to laugh. "And second, this priest is part of a very large church that I... was affiliated with for a time..." Ashleigh thought back to what the Strigoi said when he met Sebastian, as well as what Aamon said when they met. "Is this the same church that Aamon and the Strigoi mentioned?

When they each called you a 'fallen child' and 'self-righteous protestant?'" Sebastian stopped, causing Ashleigh to bump into him. "...Yes," he said bluntly. "It is the same church. And this priest is also the same man who inducted me into the church. He was a teacher of sorts to me." Ashleigh smiled. "That's great! If he was your teacher then doesn't that mean he'll be excited to see you?" Sebastian clenched his fists, not looking back at Ashleigh. "In a way yes. He will be happy to see me. But..." He paused, trying to find the words. "But what?" Ashleigh asked. "It's nothing," he finished, then continued walking. "Oh... ok," Ashleigh muttered quietly. She suddenly felt Sebastian's hands on her shoulders. "I know you want me to open up about why I can't stand to see this man," he said. "And you will know. In due time. It's just right now... I'm not ready yet. Not while dealing with Aamon. Ok?" Ashleigh looked him in the eyes. "Ok Sebastian," she said. "I'll wait. But don't make a promise you can't keep." Sebastian smiled, removing his hands and continuing to walk. "Alright then," he said. "And as for where we're going, we are heading for the commune of Ostia in Rome, Italy.

Chapter 2

Ashleigh swayed back and forth, feeling the waves kick her stomach. She began to talk, but had to hold back the vomit in her mouth. "Isn't there an easier way to traverse through the ocean," she asked. "Maybe less rickety?" another wave hit the ship, almost causing Ashleigh to lose the meal she had. Sebastian laughed, enjoying the ricketiness and the sea breeze. "It isn't so bad," he replied. "The wind blowing through your hair, the smell of the ocean in your nostrils. It's quite enjoyable at times. Would you rather have stayed behind with Aamon?" Ashleigh looked between the ocean and Sebastian. "I think I'm feeling much better actually. The breeze does smell good." Ashleigh ignored the waves and pushed her meal back down.

As Ashleigh relaxed, she looked at Sebastian and an uneasy look grew across her face. Sebastian happened to notice it. "If you are worried about me, don't be. This isn't the first time I've had to come back here. I have faced evils like this before, and I've needed help, though I usually meet others like yourself, so I haven't had to return here in a long time." Despite his remark, her look didn't change. "And yes, I'm worried. I will always be worried every time I return here. But we can't let my fear interfere with dealing with Aamon. Or helping those people." Ashleigh eased up on her worried expression, but it wasn't going to change how she felt on the inside. She was terrified for what may be causing him such distress, and all from one person. "Ok," she said. "I just want you to know that I'm here for you. And I always will be. You don't have to do this alone. You brought me along for a reason, and I want to show you that I can help." Sebastian smiled. She always found a new way to remind him for why he brought her in the first place. And he never regretted it, not even for a second. "I understand," he said. "Just don't overwork yourself doing it." Ashleigh laughed. She enjoyed her time with Sebastian, traveling and helping him in his travels. Her thoughts were interrupted by another wave, larger than the first ones before, and she lurched over the side, trying not to vomit. Sebastian laughed once more, until he was punched in the arm by a gurgling Ashleigh.

The two of them stopped talking as they closed in on their destination. The waves calmed and Ashleigh stared in awe. She was astonished by the glowing city in the morning light. The golden glow on the tops of the buildings. "Wow," she said, not taking her eyes off the city. "This is amazing. And what'd you say this place was called Sebastian?" She turned towards Sebastian, and saw that he had a look on his face. A look that reminded her of Linda when she was forced to go pay the mayor taxes back home. A look of knowing a greater good is at stake, but there's the reminder that you dread having to go. "Sebastian," she said. "Are you sure you're going to be alright?" Sebastian shook his head, as if awakening from a dream. "Oh," he said. "Yes I'm... I'm going to be fine. Thank you. We should be arriving shortly." Clyde nodded his head in agreement, continuing to man the helm as they neared the city. "Well," Ashleigh continued. "I asked you what the city was called again", Ashleigh asked. "Ah yes," he responded, showing a look of fascination. "This is the city of Ostia, a rather large community in Rome. In fact, it was the first colony founded by its fourth king, Ancus Marcius, who founded the city. He was a well-respected individual and put the practice of religion high on the duties of his subjects, and even successfully waged war against Latins during his reign. Though, he sadly died in the 600 BC era, leaving the city in rule to another ruler, only to have been killed by his sons, which then led to more death and succession." Ashleigh looked at Sebastian stunned. "Oh," she responded. "That's sounds... very sad. Sadder than even I would have expected. Is there really that much death in a country as beautiful as this?" Sebastian looked off in the distance, pondering the question.

"Sadly yes," he informed her. "There is much death and battle for power in this country. Many have lost their lives due to the level of greed that plagues us all as people. Pertinax, Balbinus, even Valentinian the second and Valentinian the third. They all lost their lives for reasons ranging from greed, misuse of power, or just because someone didn't like them. Ancus is one of the few who wasn't assassinated himself, dying of a natural death. A much better alternative then some." Sebastian laughed, despite this being such a dismal topic. "Why, there are some who died the worst way possible, usually done through repeated stabbings or poison. Of course, that was only reserved for those who were truly wicked. Domitian, Caracalla, Commodus, Cali…"

Sebastian looked over at Ashleigh who, during his listing of emperors who died horribly, was staring at him in both awe and concern. Even Clyde watched in disbelief as Sebastian listed off so much history in such a short time. "Sorry," he said, his face turning redder than a tomato. "I uh… didn't realize I was talking your ears off. I'll just, keep the rest to myself. It is a rather dark topic of conversation after all." Sebastian turned his attention back to the city, embarrassed that he had gone into such dark detail. Suddenly, he felt a hand on his shoulder. "You're fine Sebastian," Ashleigh said. "It's just… Where did you learn all this information from?" Sebastian's expression eased as he looked at her. "It was a common study when I was being taught here. We were expected to know everything about anything related to the country. And the topics of Assassination and Death of powerful individuals was usually the most important of them." "Why would such a dark topic be so necessary for a church devoted to god?" she asked. Sebastian twiddled his thumbs. "Well to put it simply, they wanted to teach us what not to do. We were taught to understand the faulty of those who failed prior to us. At least, that's what Maxwell spouted about anyway…" Sebastian's expression changed, going from wide eyed to agitate. "Maxwell?' Ashleigh asked. "Who is that?" "It's not important," Sebastian replied coldly. "At least not yet anyway." Ashleigh silenced herself, afraid to continue any further. She then heard Clyde cough in the background. She turned to him, and saw that he was shaking his head, urging her not to continue the conversation. She couldn't help but wonder, what was the connection between Sebastian and Clyde? They seemed so different and yet, Clyde was Sebastian's one and only means of transportation across the ocean. What connected them so well?

Her thought was interrupted by Sebastian poking her shoulder. She looked towards him, only to see that he was beaded with sweat, his palms shaking. "We're here," he said. As they reached the docks, Ashleigh saw that there were people lined up along it, viewing in awe at the mysterious strangers who had just arrived. "Clyde," Sebastian said. "You remember the spot where we usually put the boat?" Clyde grunted in acknowledgement. "Take the ship there for now. You can do as you please till we are done here. Don't cause a scene this time. I don't want to have to explain to the King Emmanuel why three bars in his capital have been ransacked with bodies lying on the floors." Clyde laughed, reminiscing of old times. He pushed the boat off the dock and went off to this spot. Ashleigh stared at Clyde, then at Sebastian. "Did he...?" Ashleigh began. Sebastian's eyes grew wide and he laughed. "Oh no, no. He didn't kill anyone. He just got a little too drunk and got in one too many fights. His majesty wasn't too keen on him doing that and I had to convince him not to put Clyde behind bars." Sebastian stepped forward, looking across the crowd. It began to dissipate, people spreading out around them. "Ah I miss the smell of the waterside canals of Ostia. It's so beautiful here don't you think?" Ashleigh looked around the nearby area, not so much mesmerized but rather surprised. There were people all around them, bustling down the paths. But they all looked at them strangely, as if the two of them were but aliens in a foreign world. "It's a rather fascinating city," she said. "But why are they all looking at us like we're criminals?" Sebastian began walking down a path that rose up a hill, forcing her to catch up. "Well let me answer your question with another question," he responded. "How would you feel if you just saw two strangers in odd clothes appear from nowhere on a strange boat? Wouldn't you be a bit suspicious of the newcomers in your home?" she pondered the thought, having not considered how these people must feel seeing newcomers in their home. And then as she looked at the people around her who, unlike her and Sebastian, were dressed in much different cloths. Some men wore what looked almost like bed sheets draped across their bodies, others wore finer clothing like the rich people Ashleigh would read about in children's books as a child. And the women all wore clothes that covered much more of their body, large bustles of fabric covering their lower halves or long dresses that showed less skin than a pair of shoes. And all the while, here was Ashleigh walking around in simple bar clothes that would most likely be more befitting of maids or bartenders. Sebastian must have sensed her newfound discomfort, as he took off his jacket and offered it to Ashleigh. She kindly took it, draping it over her shoulders.

"Now," Sebastian said. "How about we find ourselves a carriage that can take us to where we need to go." Ashleigh looked at him surprised. "I thought this was where we needed to be?" Ashleigh asked. "Where do we need to go now?" Sebastian began scanning the area, hoping to find someone who might be able to help them. "Technically," he began. "We need to go to the Basilica of Santa Maria Novella, and the closest portside town is Livorno." Ashleigh looked at him surprised. "So why didn't we just go to Livorno if it's closer?" Sebastian continued to search, until he smiled and began walking again. "Well you see," he began. "Livorno is one of the towns that Clyde had one too many scuffles in. And as a warning, the king made it so every town closest to the Basilica must check every boat captain, as well as the passengers. He doesn't want Clyde or his boat anywhere near the Basilica. So we started looking for other towns that don't check the captain and Ostia happened to be one of them." As he walked he caught a glance at a poster with a crudely drawn portrait of Clyde, to which Sebastian quickly tore it off the wall. "Or at the very least, it's the one city that won't be automatically searching for him anyway." Ashleigh glared at him, unsure of her safety. "The point is," he continued. "It's easier for us to take a carriage that can get us there in the next couple of days rather than try to risk getting caught in Livorno and dealing with guards. Which would you prefer?" Ashleigh went to respond, but decided to hold her tongue since she didn't know the area. "Exactly," he said. "Now, here we are." He gestured to a small building that rested just outside the town. It hadn't occurred to her, but they managed to walk all the way through Ostia in just a short time. The city looked large from the water, but when you walk though it it's actually quite small.

Sebastian walked up to the small building and knocked on the door. After a brief silence Ashleigh heard some scrambling from inside and then a small old man came out from the door. He had wild gray hair and a dirt covered robe on.

He looked between Sebastian and Ashleigh, then back at Ashleigh. "Cosa vuoi?" Sebastian took a breath then responded with, "Vogliamo noleggiare la vostra carrozza." Ashleigh didn't speak any Italian, so she was left out of the conversation. The two continued to banter for a few minutes, the old man at one point pulling out a large knife and started waving it at Sebastian. Sebastian managed to calm him down. Finally, Sebastian handed the old man a small pouch and began to walk away. But before he got very far the old man yelled at him one last time. He yelled, "Fammi vedere la schiena, giovanotto." Sebastian looked at him skeptical. "Se non lo fai, allora non ti aiuterò," the old man continued while waving the small pouch back and forth. "Bene Bene," Sebastian said, beginning to walk back. Ashleigh watched as Sebastian lifted up the back of his shirt, revealing something that mad the old man cover his mouth. He turned Sebastian around, letting his shirt fall down; then, he placed his right hand on his forehead and mumbled something that Ashleigh could not here, despite not even being able to understand it.

The old man made one final remark and then walked around behind the building. "Well?" Ashleigh asked. "What on earth did you two talk about?" Sebastian rubbed his head, trying to come up with the words. "Well," he began. I asked him if we could hire his carriage to take us where we needed to go, to which he got enraged by the location and began swinging a knife. I finally told him he doesn't have to take us all the way, at least up to a mile away from the church. And so he finally agreed and he went to get a carriage with two horses. Said it should only take two or three days." Ashleigh nodded. "What about that bit at the end where you lifted the back of your shirt? What was that about?" Sebastian's expression changed, turning to a slight grimace. "...Its nothing. Really. Just an old man being odd is all. Come on, let's meet with him before he decides to run off with his payment." The two of them followed the man's footsteps to the back of the building, only to find a very old and very rickety carriage. There were two horses tied to the front, each with soft looking brown fur and long black manes. Ashleigh couldn't help but be mesmerized by the horses, having never seen any as beautiful as these before. "Wow," she said, walking up to them. "They're gorgeous." "Never saw many horses in Ireland I take it?" Sebastian asked. Ashleigh had become mesmerized by the equestrians. "No, not really. All we ever had out there were Connemara Ponies here and there, and even then there weren't many where I lived as the only ones around belonged to the farmers outside of town. But this is amazing."

"Thank you," a voice said. Ashleigh turned to see the old man poking his head from outside the carriage door. "I bred them myself, and I take great pride in them." He got out of the carriage and walked up to one of the horses, placing his hand on its muzzle. "You speak English?" Ashleigh asked. "Yes," the old man replied. "I am old and I have learned many things through my life, so I know your language." He looked at the horse and began petting its muzzle. "It's sad how common these two are out here, as most everyone has seen a horse like this." The horse nuzzled its master's hand, urging him to pet the creature further. "To others, a Calabrese is just another horse. But to you, this is a one of a kind. And I am greatly appreciative." He let the horses muzzle go and walked back towards the building. He walked around for a moment, as if searching for something, until he looked down and pulled out a set of reins. "I apologize for not speaking to both of you before," he continued as he prepared the reins. "I am naturally skeptical of others, as most people do not come to me for any business. So to see people like you to appear at my doorstep surprised me to say the least. So I was hesitant and made sure you weren't bad people." As he finished the reins, he took a look at Sebastian. "To be fair, your friend here did appear in 'their' clothes." Ashleigh looked at Sebastian, and then at his coat that she was now wearing. "What do you mean?" Before Sebastian could answer, the old man cut in again. "Men have secrets. Some they choose not to say. You're friend has a story that he is fearful to tell you." He hopped up the front of the carriage and placed his hands on the roof of the cart. "But he will tell you in time." He smiled at the two. "You are good people. I see that now.

"Now, let us be on our way," the old man said, adjusting himself to a better position on the seat of the carriage. Sebastian walked up and opened the door, gesturing for Ashleigh to enter first. As she placed her hand on the carriage door, she felt Sebastian place a hand on her shoulder. "I'm sorry," he said, unable to look her in the eyes. "I promise I'll tell you everything in due time. I just…" He was cut short by Ashleigh lifting his head to look him in the eyes. "It's alright Sebastian," she said with a smile. "I know you'll tell me when you're ready. For now, let's just get this all sorted out. Together." The two smiled at each other, then climbed into the carriage. "I hope you two didn't eat any big meals before this," the old man yelled from outside. "The road ahead is a bumpy one, and I hope you're ready." Sebastian looked between Ashleigh and the window of the carriage door. "Yes," he said quietly. "Yes it is a bumpy road."

Chapter 3

"Are we there yet?' Ashleigh said over the sound of rocks under the carriage wheel. "It's been four days, with the wheel almost breaking 9 times. "How much longer will it be until we arrive?" Sebastian stared out the window admiring the scenery. "You complain too much," he said with a smile. "You should take in the surroundings, look at how beautiful the country side is." Ashleigh looked out the window of the carriage once more, looking at this scenery that Sebastian was so entranced by. "Yes Sebastian, it is beautiful," she said as another hill passed by. "But I've also been staring at it for four days. It finally got boring within the second day. I don't understand how you can enjoy this so much since all we really see are hills and the occasional town here and there." The old man chimed in from the front. "You look too deeply into it young girl. You must not look at what you see directly, but rather feel it around you. Feel the peace that surrounds us and embrace it." She looked at the wall that was the old man's voice, unsure how to answer. "What he means," Sebastian said. "Is that you shouldn't be looking into what you see so much. Just take a deep breath, and feel the air around you."

Ashleigh didn't see a point in what they were saying, but she felt she should give it a try. She sat still and closed her eyes, taking in a deep breath. She took in everything around her. The sound of the rocks under the carriage wheels, the smell of the horses, even the sound of Sebastian's breathing. The less she dug deep into her surroundings and just simply took them in, she could feel a sense of peace. She could even make out the sound of her own heartbeat. "You know, I guess it is rather nice," she said. "When you take in the silence, it just feels... peaceful." Sebastian looked at her and grinned, almost as if everything that was troubling him had finally left, at least for a moment. "Told you so," he said.

Their moment of peace was cut short by the sound of the horses whinnying loudly, followed by a sudden stop. "Is everything alright out there?" Sebastian yelled. "What happened?" For a moment there was only silence, and then, all the old man said were three words. "We are here." Sebastian and Ashleigh each exited the carriage to see what the old man had encountered, and to their shock it was more than they expected.

They had finally reached the location of the Basilica, and Ashleigh couldn't help but be impressed. The city they were looking at spread out for miles, buildings as far as the eye could see. Ashleigh had never been to such a large city, and couldn't help but wonder if she'd ever get another chance. "Well, this is where we part ways I suppose," the old man said. Ashleigh turned around and saw that the old man was staring off at the city, and Ashleigh couldn't figure out whether or not the man's expression was one of discomfort or longing. It was as if he wanted to go to the city, but the thought of being there made him sick. "This is as far as I go, but I wish you two the best of luck." The old man jumped down from his seat and stuck his hand out to Sebastian, who kindly shook it in thanks. He then walked over to Ashleigh and offered the hand. Ashleigh took his hand and shook it firmly, thankful that the old man brought them this far. "And young man." He looked to Sebastian, who had been staring at the city. He turned and Ashleigh couldn't help but think that he had the same expression the old man had. "Tell him to come visit me some time," he said, his face growing sad. Sebastian took a moment to respond, but he gave the man his word that he would deliver the message. And with that, the old man took off in his carriage, returning to Ostia. Just before he passed over a hill, the old man turned and waved at the two travelers. As Ashleigh waved back, she looked to Sebastian and saw that he was looking at the old man sadly, as if he felt bad for him. "Hey Sebastian," Ashleigh said. He looked at her, shaking his face and giving her a friendly smile. "Yes?" he responded. "What was that bit about telling him to visit the old man? Do you two know someone in common?" Sebastian hesitated to answer, but simply said that he happened to know a friend of the old man, and he asked that he tell him to visit sometime. Choosing not to push the topic any further, they began walking to the city. After a few minutes, Sebastian began looking around nervously. "Hmm," He said to himself. "Thought they would've been here by now. They don't normally let me get this close without charging towards me." "Who would've been here by now?" Ashleigh asked.

Suddenly, an army of men appeared from nowhere, circling the two and creating a wall around them. They wore clothes similar what Sebastian was wearing, but instead of carrying a book they carried swords and rifles. "That's who should've been here by now," he said. Ashleigh stood there confused, deciding to do the only thing she could do; put her hands in the air and wait. Sebastian stepped forward, and spread out his arms. "Well it's so good to see you all again," he said. "Luca, Mobius, good to see you. I hope you've done well. How is his lordship of the church?" The men all looked at him silently, not responding, each with a unique glare of hatred. "No response? Well I would've thought you'd be glad to see and old friend." "You are no friend to this Country Sebastian!" A voice yelled

across the mass of soldiers. The army seemed to instinctively part ways, making an open path. At the end of the path, was a man. He looked no younger than Ashleigh and Sebastian, possibly of 19 years. He had long blonde hair put back in a ponytail. His clothes resembled Sebastian's, but were pure white, with a red cross running across the front. He carried a sword unfamiliar to Ashleigh, with a crescent guard and a long thin blade, which glowed in the sunlight. He had a stern look for someone his age, seeming like he had faced many hardships in such little time. "Why are you here?" he asked. His voice had a strong accent, reminding her of the old man from the carriage.

"Johnny!" Sebastian yelled. "My have you grown in these few years. How old are you now, 17? 18? Last I recall you were still only a young boy, training with a wooden blade. You grew out of the training clothes I see..." He was interrupted by this Johnny pulling out his sword, and pointing it at Sebastian's neck. The tip was nearly an inch from piercing his throat. "Cease your chattering dog," Johnny said, growing agitated. "And stop referring to me by that damned nickname. Speak to me as Sir John from now on. Understand?" Sebastian nodded his head. "You got it Johnny." John grumbled, moving the tip closer to Sebastian's neck. "Why are you even here? What business could you possibly have in this country? I thought you learned your lesson last time." Sebastian smiled, moving the sword away with his finger. "Well you see," he began. "As much as I didn't want to return here, I had to." Sebastian paused a moment. "I... We... need your help." John looked confused, but then lowered his sword. He looked back at Ashleigh. She smiled as best she could and waved at him. "Hello," she said, trying not to lose her sense of control. John looked between the two of them for a moment, and then sheathed his sword. "Alright," he said. "You can see his graciousness. But I'm not letting you out of my sights. Understand?" Sebastian smiled like a boy, and placed his hands in his pockets. "Understood Sir Johnny," he said. Sir John looked more enraged now, flexing his fist near the handle of his sword. "I said, don't call me that," he mumbled under his breath. "Follow us. And guards, keep an eye on them from the back." They began to walk forward. Ashleigh made sure to stay close to Sebastian, as to not risk angering the guards. "What did you do to anger him so much?" Ashleigh asked. "I mean other than call him Johnny." Sebastian smiled at Ashleigh, and looked back at John. "Oh he's not that bad. He just has a funny way of showing he misses me. Sir John turned his back and glared at Sebastian. "Don't think I won't kill you Sebastian. I'm not nearly as tolerant of your attitude as Maxwell." Ashleigh immediately caught the name, and her mouth acted before her brain. "Who is Maxwell?" she asked, just before immediately covering her mouth.

Sebastian turned to her, his look of pleasure towards teasing John was replaced with a look of terror. Sir John quickly lifted his hand, signaling for his men to stop. He turned around, looking at Sebastian shocked. "You mean you didn't tell her?" he asked. Sebastian took a deep breath and turned his attention back to the front. "I *was* getting around to doing it," he said giving Ashleigh a minor glare. "But as we all know, I am not exactly on the best terms with Maxwell. So I was hesitant to start talking about him." The men surrounding them began muttering to one another, keeping their words to themselves. All Ashleigh could hear were the repeating words of 'traitor' and 'embarrassed'. Sir John signaled his hand in the air again, silencing his men. "Well then," he replied. "I suppose she will get to see for herself an unbiased view of Maxwell." He began walking again, and Ashleigh felt a rifle bump into her back. "It'll be good for her to make her own mind on how she sees Maxwell, rather than her view be decided by your attitude, Sebastian." Sebastian ducked his head down, placing his hands in his pockets. "I'm sorry Sebastian," Ashleigh stated trying to make him feel better. "I didn't mean to just say that, it just sort of happened and..." Sebastian interrupted her by lifting his hand. "It's fine," he said. She couldn't help but get more concerned at his response, feeling no emotion from his words. "John is right I suppose. Better for you to have your own opinion of Maxwell then have it be based off of my own." He turned his head back to ground beneath his feat. "Come on," he said. "Let's get this over with." And with that, they continued walking.

Chapter 4

As they walked through the city, people stared at them curiously. Then again, Ashleigh couldn't blame them. She couldn't very well blame anyone for wanting to look at the two strangers that were being escorted by a mass of guards. They walked for what seemed like hours, adding in the constant glare of eyes. As they walked, Ashleigh made sure to stay close to Sebastian, as to not get too close to the guards. She continued to look between the guards and Sir John. Sebastian said that John was nothing to really worry about, as he supposedly 'showed his feelings in unique ways.' She chose not to risk angering the young man so she made sure to keep her distance. All the while, Sebastian never said a word, occasionally tapping his hands to his pockets, almost like a nervous tick. She didn't understand why he hated it here so much, or why he couldn't bear to talk about Maxwell to her. But what she did understand was he needed someone by his side, even if that someone was the very person who brought up Maxwell.

"We're here," John said. Ashleigh looked up to see a tall building with large rounded roofs and a tower standing above the rest. The building and its surrounding area were twice the size of her hometown, and looked even older as well. The rooves were decorated with red tiles and the walls were painted white and had intricate designs painted all across the building. She couldn't help but be amazed by such an astounding building. But, her wonder was soon cut short as she felt the group stop suddenly. She barely kept herself from bumping into the guards. One of them turned back to face Ashleigh, and looked between her and Sebastian. After looking at Sebastian, he turned to her, and glared her in the eyes. The glare shook to her bones, but she simply smiled back at the man. *'Why do these men hate Sebastian so much?'* she wondered while looking at the people who watched them as they walked. She couldn't help but notice that every so often there would be groups of people watching them, muttering inaudible words to one another. There would even be the occasional child here and there watching them up until their mother or father swooped them away, urging them to avert their eyes and hide indoors. *'And how could one man anger an entire church, as well as those affiliated with them?'*

"Look, Ashleigh," Sebastian said, interrupting her thoughts. She looked up at him to see he was beaded with sweat, his eyes darting back and forth between the passersby and John. "When we enter this building, I want you to stay as close to me as possible. And whatever you do, don't get into any deep conversations with Maxwell. Alright?" She was unsure about his warnings, but she wouldn't argue. He knew more right now than she did right now, and she trusted him. "Alright," she said. "I will." Without thinking, Ashleigh grabbed Sebastian's hand. It was damp with sweat, shaking in fear. Before she could pull away out of worry, Sebastian tightened his grip, pulling her close. As her face reddened, she looked at him to see that a little bit of his worry had dissipated. To think that in such short time they had grown so close.

"Guards, return to your posts," he said, not taking his eyes off them. "You needn't be burdened by such a trifle like this anymore." The guards each walked off to their own places and areas. Soon all that remained were Ashleigh, Sebastian, and Sir John, who hadn't left the door. "Sebastian…" Ashleigh began, but she was interrupted by John, who caught she was talking and decided to intervene. "Listen dog," he said to Sebastian. "You too, Irish girl." She looked at him slightly offended. "You two are to do as I say, otherwise, I will personally have you put in the stocks to be hanged. Got it?" Ashleigh silenced herself, but Sebastian nodded his head. "Yes yes," he said. "We get it, your strict and would gladly kill us. Look John, I just want to see Maxwell, and we'll be on our way. Alright?" John looked at Sebastian with a sense of hatred that Ashleigh didn't see too often. "Alright," he said, looking at them silently. "We'll go see Maxwell." "Thank you," Sebastian said. He began to walk towards the door, with Ashleigh following close behind. He placed his hand on the door. Before he could push it open, John placed his arm across his chest. "Just make sure that no one's going to kill you on your way in," he said, giving Sebastian a smirk. "I trust you remember the way to his Lords quarters?" Sebastian turned to face him, and returned the smirk. "You know for someone your age, I'm surprised that your memory is as weak as an old mans." Sebastian pushed the front door open, the door leaving a loud creaking noise.

Before she could enter, Sir John placed his hand on her shoulder. She stopped dead in her tracks. She turned to him, covering her look of terror with a simple look of confusion. "Yes?" she asked. She followed his gaze and noticed he was staring at Sebastian's journal. "You carry his book," he stated. "Why?" She wasn't sure how to answer. She wanted to just say he gave it to her but it might make him look worse than he already does. "Umm…" she stammered. She was cut off by Sebastian. "She's fine Johnny," he said. "I gave it to her. She's better at looking for important details that I take forever to find. She helps." That comment seemed to shut him up. He looked at her one more time. "Is this true girl?" she nodded. "Yep," she mumbled. She rushed over to Sebastian, following him inside. People on the other side all turned to look at the door, and all had open mouths and wide eyes as Sebastian entered. "Shall I lead you to where he is, Sir John?" John simply stood still, and nodded his head. "Why not?" he replied. "Let's see if your memory is as good as you say it is." Sebastian gave him one more smirk, and entered the grand building.

As they walked, people lined the halls, watching as the three of them walked along. Some looked at them confused, not sure as to who they were. Others, judging by the looks they had, must have known who Sebastian was, as they gave him dirty looks and mumbled to each other. Ashleigh was still concerned as to what Sebastian did, but her only option was to wait and find out later. She looked back towards the two men in front of her. She found it strange that as obvious as it is that Sir John hates Sebastian's insides, he seemed willing enough to joke with him, like old friends. As they walked, they soon reached a flight of stairs. They went up, walking for quite some time. *'How high are we going?'* She asked herself. Her thoughts were interrupted by the men stopping at yet another large door. It stood taller than Ashleigh, nearly reaching the immensely high ceiling. And yet it was smaller than the front entrance.

"We're here," Sir John said. He turned to Ashleigh. "Please show some respect to his lordship, Irish Girl. I will not take kindly to any of the unnecessary brutish behavior that you Irish folk are known for." Ashleigh began to get angry. "Ok I've had enough?" she said, giving the man a look. "I'll have you know that not all of us Irish folk are brutes. And second, if I feel threatened by anyone or anything, I'm going to defend myself, even if that means getting a little 'brutish' as you put it. And let's not forget that I have a name. So, I'd prefer if you referred to me as such instead of Irish Girl. Otherwise, I'd be happy to introduce you to the famous Irish temper." Sir John turned towards her, looking slightly agitated, but Ashleigh didn't care. She was sick of being talked down to. She was a person, not some stray cat. "Well then," he said. "If your partner would've introduced us properly, I wouldn't have to call you Irish girl." He turned towards Sebastian. He looked startled, unsure how to answer. "I thought you would've been a gentleman and asked her what her name was." John rolled his eyes. "Honestly, you have no manners, nor have you ever." Sir John turned back towards Ashleigh, reaching his hand out. "Since he will not do it, I will begin introductions. My name is Sir John Russo. I am a member of the Great Church. And you are?" He placed his hand out waiting to shake. Ashleigh was hesitant, but was relieved he was trying. "Ashleigh," she said placing her hand upon his. "Ashleigh Briner. Of a small tavern in Ireland; and it's good to make your acquaintance." The two shook hands. "And by the way, I am well accustomed to the old Irish temper, so you needn't worry of showing me." Sebastian stood to the side clapping. "Well," he said. "Now that that's out of the way, let's go see old Maxwell then."

Sebastian went and pushed open the door. It was silent, and opened into a large, dimly lit room, the only light being a couple of candles placed about the room. A desk sat in one corner, next to a large window, covered by a curtain, letting not much light inside. To another end there was a bed that was barely visible. It had tall bedframes, with a thin curtain on the front, keeping anyone from looking at whoever slept. And amidst the room, were multiple bookshelves, filled to the brim with books. Ashleigh tried to see the titles, but it was too dark. And any she could see were written in Italian. "Hello?" Sebastian called. "Anyone home? Maxwell it's me, Sebastian. I came because there's a problem my partner and I need your help with. And we would happily explain it to you if you'd actually show your face…"

"No need to get so hasty Sebastian," a voice said. It was low, resonating within the room. She couldn't see where it came from with the dim lighting, until she looked at the bed. Before it was empty. Now, there was a figure sitting up in the bed. Ashleigh couldn't see their face, but she knew it was an older man. His voice was deep but jagged, reminding her of a low drum. He stood up from his position and stretched his arms. "I see you haven't gotten any better at dressing yourself," the man said, turning his head towards Sebastian. Sebastian looked at himself, confused. "I don't quite know what you mean," he said, trying to hide a look of grimace under a smirk. The man at the bed laughed and began to walk towards a door. It was then Ashleigh realized he was not wearing any clothing. She quickly turned her gaze away and hid her face behind the journal. The man entered the door and continued to speak. "I mean that daft scarf," he said, throwing a piece of clothing out the door. "Honestly Sebastian. You never respected the simplicities of a Church Duster. They are a grace upon the wearer and should not be tainted with some trashy fabric." A few more clothes flew out the door.

Then, the man reentered. He wore a more pristine version of one of the many dusters the people here wore. He walked over towards the mirror at the other end of the room. As Ashleigh's eyes followed him around the room, the dim lighting of the candles let her see the detail on it. It looked old, with ornate carvings on the frame and it was attached to a small cabinet. The man pulled open a drawer and took out a black neck tie, and began setting it upon his neck. "I do believe you should introduce me to your partner. Or have you forgotten what it means to be a gentleman?" he asked, eyeing Sebastian. She turned to Sebastian who, in silence, grumbled under his breath and forced a smile. "This is my partner Ashleigh. I met her in Ireland, and she has helped me deal with a Strigoi I had been searching for. But that isn't why we are..." He was interrupted by the man. "Really? A young girl helped you? My you must have lost more than I anticipated to have needed a young girl to help." He chuckled, sending a shiver down Ashleigh's spine. Something about him didn't seem right.

Sebastian's face began to redden, looking unpleased with the man trying to make a fool of him. "Listen Maxwell," Sebastian snapped. "I'm not here to be lectured by you like a child again. I only came here because Aamon has returned and he has somehow found a way back from hell. We need your help and if all you are going to do is sit in the darkness and ridicule me, then we'll just leave you to your pompous lifestyle you old..." he was stopped by John pulling out his sword and aiming it at Sebastian. "Watch what you say," he said, keeping the blade within inches of Sebastian's throat. "I don't have time for you to be a loyal guard dog either," Sebastian said. He turned to face John. "Enough," Maxwell yelled. He spoke calmly and yet kept a violent tone. The two men, near seconds from tearing at each other's throats, both stopped. Sebastian crossed his arms and John sheathed his sword. Ashleigh had no words. She was too terrified to even move or speak. "Honestly," Maxwell began. "The two of you claim you're adults and yet you squabble like infants." The man had finished setting his tie in place and began to walk towards the three. Ashleigh noticed he was moving more towards her and she tried to move, only to realize he was going for the large window. He placed his hands on each curtain. "Aamon is a threat to both the church, and the people. We will aid you Sebastian. But…" He turned to look at Ashleigh. "This does not excuse what you have done. Nor will it ever." He threw open the curtains. Ashleigh was blinded by a bright light, and averted her eyes back to where the bed stood to let her eyes adjust. As she looked back at the bed, she couldn't help but notice a large painting resting above the bed. It had a strange man standing sideways, his face facing one direction, and yet his body was in full view. He had an oddly shaped hat on his head that was just too odd for words. She also noticed it was holding two sticks in each hand, one with a hooked end, and the other with strands of cloth hanging on the end.

Before she could look at it any further, the painting was covered up by a long shadow, she turned to see Maxwell and could finally get a good look at the man. He was older than Sebastian, maybe in his later fifties. He had long white hair and a thick beard. He stood tall and looked intimidating. Ashleigh caught his gaze. The two locked eyes and she noticed something. His eyes seemed to change for a split second and, for a moment, they were black with a red iris. Then, they returned to a normal eye the shade of blue. "Now," he said turning his gaze back to Sebastian and John. "How about we go to the main hall? It's almost time for prayer."

Chapter 5

Ashleigh couldn't seem to take her eyes off Maxwell. As they walked to the main hall from his quarters, she felt something sinister about him. He just seemed odd, carrying himself in a manner that just didn't seem very normal. Those he spoke to while they walked talked to him in a very high regard, showing a great deal of gratitude, but it didn't excuse how she felt. And those eyes. She didn't understand what she saw before, but it just didn't seem human. She tried her best to remain cool headed as they continued to walk, noticed how details the building really was. The amount of work that was put into building it alone seemed impossible, especially when considering the extra details and decorating of the building.

As they walked Ashleigh couldn't help but notice that many of the people who served the church all wore the same duster as Sebastian and Maxwell. Most of them black with a white undershirt while some had tailored white. She couldn't help but consider why there weren't others with a coat like Johns, white with the long Red Cross. She dismissed as they neared closer to the main hall she started noticing that it wasn't all men in the church, a few women and children strolling around the halls. Most women wore long black dresses that kept their bodies hidden from hull view, only showing their hands and face. Even their hair was kept in a much hidden manner, being put up into a tightly done bun with a ribbon keeping it together. Children all seemed to wear clothes similar to the adults, boys walking around in smaller dusters and girls wearing little black dresses with ribbons keeping their hair back. Ashleigh couldn't help but be in awe at how organized this church was. It would've taken her town months to even consider preparing for any god of any religion, but to make it a regular part of their daily lives? She was in awe at such dedication.

They walked for about another 2 minutes or so, until they finally reached the main hall. It appeared to be less of a hall and more of a large amphitheater, benches lined up to create this large circle surrounding a single podium. The podium is what stood out to Ashleigh, as at the podium stood behind it a rather large cross. It must have been 10 feet tall, reaching well past Sebastian's height.

Maxwell walked up the stairs that led down to the podium. "Well my guests," he said, eyeing specifically Sebastian. "I don't suppose you would care to join us for service, would you?" Ashleigh looked over at Sebastian, who seemed to be judging whether or not he really wanted to. He looked towards Ashleigh, almost pleadingly. "Well," Ashleigh began. "I suppose it would be fine. But we really do need to speak with you about Aamon. It's very important." Maxwell turned his gaze to Ashleigh, almost studying her. She couldn't shake the feeling she was a corpse being studied by a mortician. "Well," he said, turning his gaze back to Sebastian. "If Aamon is of that much importance to you, Sir John and I will make our visit short." He shot his eyes towards John, who in turn, took off the belt that was holding his sword. "Miss." He looked over to Ashleigh, who was startled by the man holding out his sword to her. "It is unfit for one to take a weapon into the place of God. Would you please hold my saber? I should not be long." Ashleigh was surprised. A man who met her no more than a couple hours prior, was trusting her with his weapon. "Y...Yes. I will hold your... what was it? Saber?" He nodded. "Right. I will hold your saber." He placed it out in front of her, waiting for her to grab. She placed her arms in the air in front of her. He placed it surprisingly gently, making sure it did not throw her off. She was flattered, but not bothered by the weight. It was surprisingly light.

As she held it, he nodded his thanks and followed Maxwell up the stairs. She watched as the two went up to the grand door. When she turned back, she saw Sebastian eyeing the two maliciously. It startled her. She wasn't used to him acting so aggressive. He must have realized she was watching him, shaking his head and turning towards her. "Right," he said, trying to act normal. "How about we take a seat? Wait for them to finish. They shouldn't be too long hopefully." Sebastian took a seat on one of the steps. "Now and then he'll take his time, but even he knows Aamon is a threat. To both the people *and* his church." He looked off in the distance, as if thinking about something. She looked ahead of him, noticing more people who stared at him like a sideshow attraction. Ashleigh sat down next to him, placing the sword on the step next to her.

"Sebastian," she started, turning to look him in the eyes. "I need to know. Why does Maxwell treat you like such a child? Why does every member of this church act as if you're some war criminal? And what did you ..." she was interrupted by Sebastian placing his hand up in front of her. "I know you want answers as to why things are the way they are here," he responded. "I know you're concerned about my wellbeing. And I'm grateful, but I need time to tell you. But right now isn't the best time. I promise, you'll know everything." He turned back towards the main center of the amphitheater. She looked in the direction, and noticed two small children watching him. They eyed Sebastian, and he eyed them. But then they noticed Ashleigh watching them, and one of the children looked at her. It was a boy, with scraggly brown hair and tattered dress clothes. But when Ashleigh went to look at his eyes, he seemed to avert her gaze. He turned towards his left, and a woman stood up. She wore a flowy tattered dress. The two spoke in silence. The mother glanced towards Ashleigh, then pulled the children away, cutting through the crowd.

"Wonder what bothered them..." Ashleigh began, until she noticed Sebastian eyeing her. He looked oddly confused. "What?" Sebastian looked away, trying to hide his expression. "N-Nothing," he said. "Just thought it was odd. Usually they only stare at me. Guess they thought you were interesting." Ashleigh turned back and looked at the ground. "Yeah," she said, glancing back and forth at him. "I guess."

After a few minutes of prayer and sermon, a large mass of people began piling up the stairs, forcing Ashleigh and Sebastian to step aside. As people walked past them up the steps, they gave Sebastian dirty looks. Some glanced at Ashleigh curious, but never troubled her. It was as if Sebastian was all they cared about. "Well that was a wonderful service," Maxwell said, following behind the large crowd with John behind him. He reached the top and turned back to face them. "I do so wish you two could've joined us. It would've been more extravagant. Perhaps you could've spoken a few words my boy." He looked over at Sebastian. "I don't think that's the best," he responded. "I'm not always the best with crowds." Ashleigh wanted to say something, but thought it wasn't best time. John walked up to her. "May I have my sword back miss?" Ashleigh looked at him startled, then nodded her head and handed him his sword. "Thank you," he said. "I'm thankful no one tried to steal it from you. Most would've seen a young girl with a weapon and saw it as a chance to take it." Ashleigh didn't know whether to be flattered or offended. "Well, even if someone were to, I do know how to fight. I'm not helpless." John looked at her, judging whether to believe her. "Yes," he said. "Thank you. I don't trust many with this." He eyed the sword like it was the only thing in the world.

Before she could continue to ponder, her thoughts were interrupted by Maxwell speaking up. "Well," he said with a grin. "I'm famished. What do we say about getting some food? The Morte Deum should begin serving soon..." He was stopped by Sebastian, who stepped up and placed his hand out. "Listen Maxwell, we don't have time," he said. "We need to talk about Aamon. I can't sit here as you waste time with this. He's an issue and we need to take care of it. Now." Maxwell stood there, silent but smirking. Ashleigh was getting concerned. For as long as she had known him, Sebastian has never gotten as aggressive as he had been recently. It started to worry her. "Listen, Sebastian," she started. "Maybe we should leave. This isn't going well. We should..." Before she could continue, Maxwell raised his arms in the air. "Yes of course!" he stated. "We mustn't forget why you came here. He is a major concern and we should deal with him. But in due time. It has been a long while since you've been here. And there are those who would be ecstatic to see you. Don't you think?" Sebastian looked very hesitant. "That may be so, but still..."

Maxwell cut him off with an arm around the shoulder. He bumped into Ashleigh, sending her backward. She would've nearly fallen on her bum if John hadn't been behind to stop her. She looked up and him, and caught a glimpse of a smile. "Thank you," she said. He nodded. She adjusted herself and saw that Maxwell had begun walking away with Sebastian, pulling him along with his arm. "Now, if we have a meal, it will get you acquainted with those around you once more. It will be fine." Sebastian continued to look worried, but he realized there was no getting out of it. "Al...Alright. I suppose so. But not for long. We need to discuss this." Maxwell laughed, seeming pleased with his compliance. "There you go," he said. "Now, let us go to the Morte Deum." Maxwell continued to pull Sebastian along, and all he could do was turn to Ashleigh with a pleading look that said *Help me.*

As she began to walk, John stopped her. She turned around to see him with a concerned look, eyeing the two men ahead of them. "What is it?" she asked. "Is everything alright?" He continued to look ahead, not taking his eyes off Maxwell. "I know Sebastian is concerned with you speaking with me and Maxwell. But I give you my word. I mean no harm. And I find it odd that his grace is so caring towards him." He tilted his head down, trying to hide his voice but failed. "Even with what he's done." Ashleigh saw a chance and took it. "What did he do to make this city hate him so?" she asked. "You treat him as a black sheep or an enemy of the state." He looked at her, contemplating what to say. "I'm afraid I'm not the one to say. That is for your friend to do." He began to walk, trying to catch up to the others. "But I will say this," he said. "It may not seem as bad at first, but when he tells you, you should really consider it. And then, you may understand." And with that, he walked along, with Ashleigh following, even more confused than before.

Chapter 6

Ashleigh didn't think that she could be any more amazed by the city than she already was, until she saw the Morte Deum. It was larger than the amphitheater the service was in, with open walls held up with pillars and a set of large stone steps going up. Each pillar was carved beautifully, bearing no marks of imperfection what so ever. She wondered who it was to craft such remarkable buildings all over this city. "You certainly expanded the building, didn't you Maxwell?" Sebastian said, looking over the large building. "Well," he began. "The more people join the church, the more room we needed. And there are still those who live in the shallows who need our help. So, we built it further along to make room." Ashleigh was startled. To think this giant building wasn't even always this size.

As they climbed the stairs, Ashleigh looked onward, noticing more and more people lining the outside of the building. They all eyed the group with different reactions. Most looked at Maxwell and John with a sort of reverence or respect; others looked at Sebastian with wonder or disgust; and finally, the few who looked at Ashleigh just saw her and looked confused. It was as if they could not place who she was with or why she was here.

When they finally reached the top of the stairs, Ashleigh looked up in awe at the buildings height once more. It seemed to reach unimaginable heights, heights that she didn't think were attainable by men and women of today. As they entered, people and groups walked past them talking; they made slight glances toward them, but did not act out too much. Entering the Morte Deum, she began to notice an assortment of aromas. Scents of seasons she had known of and used and others she had never even smelt before. They continued to follow the smell and she finally saw where it came from. Inside the Morte Deum it was a long open hall, with tables big and small spanning across the floor. At the far ends there were long rectangular tables lined with an assortment of food and drinks she had never seen before. It got to a point to where Ashleigh became more amazed by the food then anything.

Sebastian seemed to catch her wonderment and laughed. She turned to him, her cheeks blushing. "What's so funny?" she asked. He calmed himself down enough to answer, but not enough to hide a smirk. "It's nothing," he said. "It's just, you remind me of a young child entering a store full of sweets. So amazed at the assortment you don't know where to start." She continued to blush and punched him in the arm. "Well excuse me for being used to simple things. Not all of us get to enjoy feasts fit for the Queen of England." She was interrupted by Maxwell laughing. He turned around and eyed the two. "Oh please my dear," he said. "The Queen wishes she was as capable at making feasts like this." Sebastian seemed to lose his aggression towards Maxwell for a moment, laughing with him. "That may be true. But the English do know their pastries. You must at least give them that." Maxwell thought for a moment, then shrugged his arms. "I suppose," he said. "Then again, you would also know that, considering where I found you in your youth. My, you were so young it seems like it was just yesterday you were…"

Maxwell stopped when he noticed that Sebastian had loss his sense of joy. His look became aggravated, eyeing Maxwell with a look of distaste. "I asked you to not speak of my life there," he mumbled. Ashleigh grew concerned. He was upset before but it seemed he had reached a new level. "My boy," he began. "I had assumed you had matured past this. Surely you've moved on from then and you can look back on it as if it was a phase or memory." He went to place his hand on his shoulder, but Sebastian snatched himself away. "No, you don't understand," he stammered, his voice shaking. "You've always said I need to move past it but I cant. It was a part of my life that I cannot move past and it's burned in my mind." His voice began to louden, drawing the attention of onlookers. Ashleigh felt uneasy, sensing that many of the surrounding folk were ready for a fight, noticing they placed their hands in their coats. "Sebastian," she started, not removing her eyes from the others. "Maybe we should…" She was interrupted by John placing his hand on her shoulder. She turned back to see a look on his face. She expected him to have been like the other onlookers, angry at Sebastian for shouting at their prophet and leader. But instead, he had a look of both concern and pity. He had his hand by the hilt of his blade, keeping his eyes not on Sebastian, but on Maxwell. It was as if he was more worried that the old man would try something before anyone else would.

"I've been trying to forget about my old life for the past 5 years," Sebastian continued. "And I have yet to move on. You think it is so easy to move on, ignore everything you've done once before and act as if you're some perfect Godsend. Well you're not. No one is. And it's about time you realize that, and stop acting like a pompous piece of shi…" He was cut off by a fist flying at his face, landing in his nose. He fell to the floor by Ashleigh's feet. Ashleigh looked for the one who threw the fist, and saw it belonged to a scrawny and pale man with blading hair. He looked ready to kill Sebastian. "Don't you speak those words to our savior," he stammered. He was frail, and his hand looked battered from that one punch. It seemed like he put all he had in it, just to silence Sebastian. She leaned down to pick him up as the man continued. "He has done more for this country than anyone else. Especially more than you. You left us. You left to be some wandering tool for the weak people in other countries, for those who can handle themselves. All the while, people in your own home country, starve and die. And then you return to ridicule the man who has saved us; he is a blessing and you need to realize that." Once he stopped, Ashleigh took her chance. "Sebastian," she whispered. "We should leave. This isn't going so well, and I think most of the people here are ready to add a few extra punches on top of that one." He looked ready to take them all on, as if he had done this before. But when he turned to face her, he saw a genuine concern for not only his health, but for his well-being overall. She didn't want him to get hurt.

He looked at the floor, regretting what he had put her through, and he stood up, wiping the blood from his nose. "I… I'm sorry," he stammered. It not only sounded forced, but it looked forced as well. "We will leave. We've stayed our welcome, and we will take our leave." Sebastian began walking away from the crowd, only to be stopped by John's hand. "Sebastian," he said. "You can't leave yet. What about Aamon?" Sebastian turned to look at John, his face red and his eyes cold. "I've stayed my welcome here, you and I both know that. I'd rather do what I can on my own to stop Aamon than stand her any longer, waiting for Maxwell to come off his high horse." He continued walking, turning only once to salute John and Maxwell. "Good to you see you John.

You know where to find me if you need me." As they walked, she turned around to see the crowd dissipating, with Sir John speaking to the man who punched Sebastian. He glanced towards Ashleigh, looking almost regretful. She started to realize that as much as John claimed to hate Sebastian, he might have actually cared. She dismissed the idea and returned her focus to getting Sebastian out of the city. She also looked over to see Maxwell eyeing the two. He didn't look bothered by anything that happened. It was as if he enjoyed seeing the anger in both his people and Sebastian. He had a smile on his face, which terrified her more than anything. He was done with this city, and even more so of this strange old man. She decided it was time to leave.

Chapter 7

It took them almost two weeks to return to Ostia. They weren't able to find a carriage that went directly from the Basilica to the city, so they had to hop from one carriage to the next. It had taken them so long that by the time they had arrived the moon had reset from full to gone. Sebastian had been quiet for most of the trip, keeping to himself and taking care of his face from the punch. Whenever Ashleigh tried to comfort him or make him feel any better, he would just distance himself, saying he just needed some time. Ashleigh couldn't help but wonder, how could such a beautiful country with wonderful people and beautiful surroundings, be filled with so much conflict and hate. And all of it focused around one man. A man she had grown to know as kind and heartfelt and had gone on so many wondrous yet terrifying journeys with.

The more she tried to understand it the more she had a hard time piecing together any of it with the lack of detail she had, so she decided to leave it be till they were done with this nightmare all together. When they finally got to the city, they had to walk for a few hours to reach the spot that Sebastian was to meet Clyde at. He said this was done solely for the fact that Clyde knew there were those who wouldn't like seeing strangers on a strange boat, so he always made sure to hide it. Ash they got closer to their destination; Ashleigh could feel the tension rising. "Ashleigh," Sebastian said. She looked up at him. She held in a snicker, trying not to laugh at the fact that after days of healing, his nose was still blue from the punch. "I wanted to properly apologize. I shouldn't have put you through this. Through any of this. If I could have just controlled myself for one day I…" Ashleigh stopped him from walking and hugged him. "Shut up you big fool," she said, trying to hide tears. "I've may have only known you a couple of months, but I know that everything you do and say is for an honest cause. And if something is wrong and people treat you like a monster, then I'll be a monster with you. I know who you are, even if I don't know everything." She let go and looked him in the eyes. "I didn't meet this version of you that everyone hates, so until I one day do, I will still trust you. And I know you're sorry. But I won't push you to tell me why. I know you'll tell me when you're ready. OK?" Sebastian looked in her eyes. He saw an innocence. An innocence that has barely survived hardships of its own, and yet it chooses to still care for those with no innocence left. But above all else, he was reminded once more why he brought her along. And he never regretted it. Not even for a second.

"Well isn't that sweet?" a voice said through the shadows. Sebastian's head snapped up, searching for the voice. Ashleigh hid behind him, clutching her journal. "Who's there?" Sebastian said. "Show yourself." It was silent for a few seconds, until a silhouette appeared. It entered the light of the hanging lantern, revealing itself to be the man who had previously punched Sebastian in the nose. "Well if it isn't the gentleman who kindly introduced my nostrils to his knuckles. What can we do for you?" he exited his hiding spot completely and revealed he wasn't alone.

Two large men wearing the church attire followed behind him, carrying planks of wood. One had a few rusty nails poking out of it. "Sebastian…" Ashleigh mumbled. "I don't like this…" she was cut off by a hand grabbing her shoulder. It pulled he back. She felt her back against a large chest. Before she could react, she felt a knife rest against her chest. Sebastian turned around, preparing to fight back. "Whatever you want, leave her out of this," Sebastian yelled. "She has nothing to do with anything." The three men in front of him began to close the gap between themselves and Sebastian. "Maybe so," one man to the right of the leader said. He was bald, with a goatee resting on his chin. He spoke with a scratchy voice, as if he'd been smoking. And as he spoke, Ashleigh couldn't help but notice the nasty looking chunks of brown in his teeth, further proving her theory. "But from how we see it, she looks like the type to get physically involved if we try something. So that's what's he's for." He pointed his board towards the man now holding Ashleigh. Sebastian looked to his eyes, and only saw a sickness in them.

Sebastian started to worry, fearing the worst for her. But before he could react, the leader kicked him in the stomach. He doubled over, landing on his knees. The second man with the un-spiked board swung it towards Sebastian's head, barely missing as Sebastian rolled aside. "You should never have returned here you British trash," the leader said one final time. The man with the spiked board stepped forward, preparing to swing, and all Ashleigh could do was stand there with a knife to her neck.

But before the board could hit Sebastian's head, there was a bright silver flash, with a splatter of blood. Suddenly, the man began to scream. Ashleigh looked to see his hand now resting beside Sebastian on the ground, still clutching the board. As the man stood there, now clutching the stumpy remainder of his arm, everyone stood in silence. "Honestly," a familiar voice called out from above them. "When will you idiots learn not to do these things?" then, without warning, the man holding the knife to Ashleigh's neck suddenly released her, dropping the knife. She ran over to Sebastian, kicking the nearby hand into the water. "Hey!" the man yelled, blood pouring out of his wrist. "I'm going to gouge your eyes out when I get the chance," the scrawny leader yelled. "Jimmy, why'd you let her go you idiot? Are you trying to get us…" he stopped as soon as he saw what made him release her. Behind Jimmy was the tip of the sword. He walked into the light of the lantern to show it belonged to none other than Sir John. "Sebastian," he said. "I thought you were more capable of taking care of yourself? You're not usually the type to get beaten down by a few common rift raft." Sebastian tried to stand up, with Ashleigh lending him a shoulder. "Normally," he began. "Under better circumstances, yes. But as you've seen, this isn't one of my best days." John shook his head, showing a slight grin in the night light. Ashleigh was confused at why he was there, but she was thankful for it none-the-less.

His attitude returned to a stern expression as he looked to the men on the other side of the duo. He shoved the blade into Jimmy's back, urging him to join his companions. "What is the meaning of this Constantine?" he asked, looking to the leader of the hoodlums. "You... why are you helping them?" he asked in turn. "Especially him of all people?" he pointed a finger to Sebastian. "After what he's done to the city and to its people. To Maxwell even! And yet here you are, pointing the sword to the victims rather than the enemy." John walked next to Sebastian and Ashleigh, glancing towards them to make sure they were alright. "Are you hurt miss?" he asked. Ashleigh nodded in acknowledgement, assuring him of their safety. "Thanks to you, yes," she said. He smiled, and turned to face Sebastian. "Can you fight?" he asked. "Or is this going to be like in our younger days when I was forced to keep you safe from the bullies when we were children?" Sebastian laughed, stretching his legs after getting kicked. He rubbed his stomach, glancing at Ashleigh. She looked scared and confused, unsure of what to think at this moment. "I'm fine Ashleigh. I promise." She steadily nodded, stepping back to let them do their work.

Sebastian turned back to John, smiling at his previous remark. "I don't think that's how it went," he said cracking his knuckles. "If memory serves me correctly, and it does, I was the one defending you from the bullies." The two walked towards the assailant's side by side, pressing them to the end of the dock. "After all, if you were the one who saved me, that would mean you were saving me while still in an 8 year old's trousers!" John laughed at the remark, swinging his sword from side to side. "Now, I'm not that young you fool." Constantine looked to the two men with a look of confusion and terror on his face. "Why are you two like this? Constantine asked. "You two should hate each other with a passion, and yet you stand as friends. How?" The group had reached the end of the dock, their heels barely an inch from the water's edge. The two men looked at each other as John placed his sword in his sheath. "It's not a matter of whether or not I see him as a friend," John said. "It's a matter of debt. I owe him. And despite our differences, I intend to keep to that debt." John gave one final look to Sebastian, and turned back to Constantine and his associates. "Now," Sebastian said. "Do us all an immense favor, and leave us alone." He took a step towards the group, glaring at them. The largest of the men, the man who held Ashleigh at knife point, saw something in his eyes. Something to cause him great fear and make him take too far a step back. He fell towards the water, and out of instinct, he grabbed the shoulders of the other two men in the front, pulling them back into the water and leaving Constantine alone on the dock. With a splash, they swam to the surface, the two large men trying to keep the handless man afloat. "Heed this warning you scum," John said, walking closer and closer to Constantine. "Do not attack Sebastian and his companion ever again. Or so help me I'll introduce you all to the chopping block." Constantine's face grew terrified and he jumped in the water, following the already swimming group. They continued to swim, trying to get as far away from the two men as possible.

Sebastian and John stood for another moment, watching the wave's crash against the dock. "Wasn't that a tad harsh Johnny?" Sebastian asked. "I mean they should be punished in some way, but the chopping block? I never placed you for the execution type." John looked at him, seeming a bit offended. "Did you forget my sense of humor Sebastian?" he said. Sebastian's eyes got wide. "When did you ever have one to start?" John gave him a look, and the two began arguing. As they bantered, Ashleigh looked down at the book, and then to the water, wondering what was going on.

Her thoughts were interrupted by John calling her name. She shot up and looked up at him. "Hmm?" she muttered confused. "What is it?" John was holding his hand, as if waiting. "I said, are you going to come with us or not? We are going back to where you found Aamon." Ashleigh was startled, unsure of his out of the blue offer of assistance. "Why are you helping us? Didn't Sebastian basically deny all help from you people?" Sebastian looked at clouds and began whistling. John glanced at him then back at Ashleigh. "He denied Maxwell's help," he clarified, though it still didn't make much sense to her as she thought he was his right hand. "But as I said before to those fools. I owe Sebastian a debt, and I intend to keep it." He looked up in the direction out towards the city in the direction of the Basilica, but then turned back to face her.

"Now," he said turning back to Sebastian. "We should go off to retrieve that burly friend of yours and be on our way." John walked back towards the end of the dock, turning right to continue along the path. Ashleigh laughed to herself, thinking it rather funny those goons never noticed the hidden part of the dock. She noticed Sebastian standing still, looking out at the water. "Hey," she said, trying to snap him out of his trance. He shook his head, turning to face her. "Oh, sorry," he said faking an obviously forced smile. "We should follow. I just hope he knows where he's going." He walked to the end and stood, waiting for Ashleigh to follow him. Thinking for a moment, she decided to suppress the many questions she wanted to ask the two men, and ran after him, forcing an equally fake smile.

When they arrived at the boat, Ashleigh noticed that Clyde was hanging over the side of the boat. He looked ready to fall out until John ran onboard and caught him, moving him by the helm and resting him in place. "Is he alright?" Ashleigh asked. John placed his hand in front of him mouth, checking to see if he was breathing. After a moment, he set Clyde down on the deck and turned to face the two. "He's alright," he said. He went to sniff his hand and wretched back. "Ugh. Although by the smell on my hand it seems he drank too much alcohol it seems. The fool smells like an old barrel of expired whiskey." Ashleigh laughed to herself, noticing Clyde tossing and turning, mumbling about some talking cat taking his booze.

Before she could consider his dream further, her thought was interrupted by John doing something. He walked to the helm of the ship and began messing with a strange set of nobs at the helm that Clyde usually kept under his watch. After turning another nob or two, a billow of smoke escaped a small smokestack she had never noticed till now. She was surprised at how she had never noticed the boat like this. "How is the boat…" she began to ask but was cut off by Sebastian. "It's because this is a steamboat," he answered. "But the reason you didn't know, is that Clyde rarely uses the steam engine underneath in the bottom of the ship. It's mainly for whether there's no wind or if we are in a hurry." She looked at the floor of the boat. "I thought that was just a big furnace he used to cook and dry clothes." He turned to her and hid a grin. "Well yes, it is used for that. But its main purpose is to power two small water mills underneath the boat." He changed his gaze from Ashleigh back to John. "But here's what I want to know. How on earth do you know how to use a steamboat Johnny? I thought old Maxwell didn't want steamboats of any kind entering near the country?" As John fiddled with the ship, he turned and glared at Sebastian, who in turn just smirked back. "You forget who you are talking to," he responded. "I don't always sit in this city you know; I have traveled myself and when I do, I meet people and learn new things. Like how to use a steamboat. Although I've never seen one this small." Sebastian walked up to John and looked down at the ships wheel. "That's because Clyde built it himself," he stated. "He took some old steamboat parts and rebuilt them in a smaller form. It's quicker in a sense, but more prone to seaside accidents. And it tends to break down, hence the sails." Ashleigh looked up at the sails, thinking back to how often Clyde would use them, and realizing how he never once used the steam engine when she first came onboard.

"Though I don't think it matters too much right now," Sebastian said. "As long as we have a captain who can steer the ship back to where Aamon is, we'll be able to finish all of this." With that John began to steer the boat away from the dock, leaving Italy behind them. Ashleigh sat on a bench that Clyde had installed when she arrived. He didn't want her to be forced to always stand, as he and Sebastian were accustomed to. She was thankful, but she never minded standing. Though it did come in handy whenever she got too seasick.

As the boat pulled from the shore, she looked back to the town of Ostia once more and was amazed by what she saw. Even though there weren't many light sources around the town, not counting a few lanterns scattered about, the sky was lit by a sky full of stars. She couldn't help but think back to the days of her youth when she and Linda would atop the bar roof, watching stars fly through the air. "It's beautiful, isn't it?" She turned around to see John standing there, watching the city with her. "Oh, hello," she stammered. John smirked, taking a seat by Ashleigh on the bench. The two sat in silence, watching as the city pulled away in the darkness of the night. "So…" Ashleigh began, trying to break the awkward silence. "Can I ask you something?" John must've known what she was going to say, as he immediately began talking. "I told Sebastian I was going to talk to you, and despite some hesitation, he allowed for it to happen, taking over the helm. So, ask away." Ashleigh began to think, trying to decide where to start.

"Well… Why do you and Sebastian act the way you do? One minute it seems as if you would rather lock him in a cell rather than help him, and the next moment you both treat each other as old friends. Why do you do this?" John sat in silence for a moment, then looked up at her. "The truth is, I would love to see Sebastian in a cell, like you say. But I also do see him as an old friend in some ways. I have known Sebastian most my life, since I was only a young boy. He was the one who introduced me to the church even." He paused, looking as if he couldn't place the words. Sebastian…Saved my life. I owe him for where I'm at today, otherwise I'd be sitting alone and barely living. And so because of this, I owe him a life debt." Ashleigh sat in silence. "Wow. I didn't realize that's what happened. But how does this explain…" She was cut off by John, who began to look angered. "But, despite this life debt, he and I both know that he broke a sacred law of the church. And he knows that my debt can only go so fa..." He was cut off by a splash of water jumping into the boat and catching him in the face. "Whoops!" Sebastian yelled from the helm. "Sorry about that! The waters got ruff for a moment there. Guess they wanted to play." He glanced backed and gave John a sort of, hybrid look of a glare and a smirk. John grumbled, wiping his face dry with his robes. Ashleigh couldn't help but laugh. Despite everything, there always seemed to be something that could make her laugh. He looked back to Ashleigh, trying to ignore Sebastian's attitude.

"As I was saying," he continued. "My debt only goes so far. Unless there are issues such as this." His expression changed, and he looked to Sebastian. "Speaking of which, you never did get to explain in detail how and why Aamon has returned. He shouldn't have been able to break the seal Maxwell put on him years ago, so how did he escape?"

"Well as you know," Sebastian began. "The only way to break a seal of God is to have a messenger of God remove the seal. And let's face it, there's no way any willing Priest would dare let a being like Aamon free. I can only imagine the horrors a man must have faced in order to be forced to remove the seal. Which in turn, implies that Aamon must have had to find a powerful enough priest to open the seal." Sebastian sat in silence for a few moments. "OK?" John asked, unsure of where Sebastian was going with his statement. "What does one priest have to do with this?" Sebastian sighed and then continued. "What this has to do with Aamon, is that he may very well be alive. And he may be able to help us. There is no way for either of us to seal Aamon away ourselves, as even doing so would very well take our lives. All we can hope for is that Aamon may have not killed the Priest who opened the seal yet. The only problem is..." John continued his sentence, knowing exactly what Sebastian meant to say. "Even if he is alive, trying to seal Aamon would very well kill him. And that's with us helping him. If he tried it himself he would surely collapse from the shear presence of Aamon, so what even is the point?" John stood up from the bench, walking towards the helm of the ship. "Even if we help this man with the seal he won't survive. To open a seal alone will surely have taken all his energy, forcing him to recover for some time. And even with months of recovery there is still no guarantee he would be able to close a seal so soon after opening one. We're better off leaving this to Maxwell and the higher order. They have the capability of finishing this, so we should just go back..."

Sebastian slammed his fist into the front wheel of the ship, causing Clyde to toss and turn. "That old fool won't do anything for us," Sebastian barked. "He would rather see the entire town set ablaze with Aamon and the people inside. And even then, that wouldn't do anything, as he would just move on." John tried cutting him off, saying that Maxwell could close the seal with the higher order, but Sebastian just shook his head. "The Higher order is no match for a demon of Aamon's caliber and you know it. And with Maxwell in his current state of old age and having never left that damn high horse of his, he would rather send a firing squad. No, what we need to do, is find the priest who opened the seal, and help him close it. And hopefully, he might be able to survive." John shook his head. "Honestly Sebastian, even you must realize that one village doesn't mean anything in the grand scheme of things when compared to Aamon. A few people die every day for the sake of making sure others live. Honestly it's like when we were younger and you chose not to end a couple of measly lives..."

Sebastian snapped away from the wheel and grabbed John by the collar, thrusting him against the edge of the ship. Ashleigh bolted up, shocked at Sebastian's sudden burst of rage. "Don't you dare speak of them. You know damn well why they meant something to me. I wouldn't kill innocents once in my life, and I'll be damned if I let you convince me to kill an entire village." Ashleigh wanted to intervene but was too scared to even move. "Sebastian," John said calmly, trying to steady himself from falling over the side. "I understand what they meant to you, but this is different. These people, they aren't nearly as important as Aamon. If one village is what it takes to make sure that he doesn't start a panic..."

"What did I just say?" Sebastian said as he tightened his grip, his knuckles turning white. "I will not take an innocent life. Especially the innocent lives of an entire village. These people did nothing to deserve this fate, and I plan on making sure they live to see the next day. Even the priest who started all of this. Do you understand John?" The two men stood in silence, neither making a move nor even saying a word. "I said..." Sebastian continued. "I know what you said you redheaded fool," John said moving Sebastian back. "If you are this determined to not take an unnecessary life, then all I can do is go along with whatever plan you have in mind." Sebastian eased up, backing away from John. "Alright," he said, dusting off his coat. "Thank you. And please, don't bring them up again." John simply nodded his head and returned to where he was standing before. She slowly sat back down, her body shaking. *'What in God's name just happened?'* she thought to herself. *'It's as if he's two different people. One, a kind man who wants to save the lives of everyone around him.*

And another, a man filled with secrets and wants nothing more than for those closest to him to know none of them.'

Sebastian looked at her, noticing the look on Ashleigh's face. "You should both get some rest. I can man the helm for some time until Clyde gets up." He kicked Clyde slightly, causing him to toss and turn. He mumbled about the booze cat one more time and went back to sleep. "You two don't need to stay up, so get some rest. It's at least three days back. Not to mention the two days of walking through a desert." He looked to Ashleigh specifically, nodding his head. She hesitantly nodded back and climbed down to the lower deck where Clyde always kept a cot in place for her. She laid herself down and, as she did, she could hear Sebastian and John talking again, in much quieter tones. She couldn't make out many words, but she understood why Sebastian wanted her to rest. He had much to tell John that she wasn't ready for. So, she closed her eyes, hoping that one day Sebastian would trust her the same way he trusts John.

Chapter 8

Ashleigh gasped for air, breathing heavy from the scorching heat. "I really hate this," she said. "Aren't there better means of going through this desert? I get the three, almost four-day trip by boat, I understand that. But isn't there a much easier way of traversing the desert? Maybe a carriage or something? I don't understand why all we can do is ride these..." she looked down at the rather disgusting camel she was riding on. "Disgusting animals. I think I've met rats with better hygiene." Sebastian looked up from his map and back at Ashleigh, a smile growing across his face.

"Now there's no need to be so mean to the poor thing," Sebastian said. "Honestly, these animals do their best to carry us across this hot desert, and all you can do is complain. Why do you not like them?" Ashleigh pulled the reigns on the animal, trying to keep it from wandering off in some alternate direction. "It tries to bite me, has eaten through three muzzles and reigns somehow, and it tries to get close to me when we stop for water." Sebastian looked at her confused. "So?" She looked down at the camel and pointed down towards its lower regions. "It tries to get CLOSE to me Sebastian... every... single... time. And I'm getting sick of it." Sebastian looked down at where Ashleigh was pointing, and with wide eyes he started laughing incoherently. "Why is it so funny?" Ashleigh complained. "Let's see you try to keep a camel from mounting you while you get a sip of water." As Ashleigh went to open her canteen, her camel made an odd grumbling sound that made her shudder uncomfortably. "See?" she said worryingly. Sebastian laughed once more as she looked down, afraid to make any other moves. "If you two are done fooling around?" John said as he passed them. "I would like to ensure that a demon general doesn't begin wandering around trying to kill innocent people. Agreed?" Ashleigh and Sebastian both quieted themselves and tried to catch up to John as he continued forward.

As the three continued to walk, Ashleigh couldn't help but think to the other day on the boat. She watched as Sebastian and John bantered back and forth, thinking only of the history the two men shared. Despite arguing so many times, as well as threats towards one another, the two of them still acted as if they had no issues greater than who should be leading the group. Ashleigh trusted Sebastian with her life and her past... but she also thought he could trust her with his past and his problems as well. She was so lost in thought that she didn't even notice the group had stopped, almost running into them. "What's going on?" she asked. She looked to see Sebastian staring ahead wide eyed, and John covering his mouth with his hands. She followed their gaze and saw the very horror that stopped them in their tracks.

They had finally arrived to the city, but in place was now less of a city and more of a wasteland. Smoke rose above the buildings and screams could be heard from a distance. She was shocked at how much chaos one demon could cause. Sebastian jumped off his camel and walked a few paces forward, only to stop and kneel down. She saw him pick up what looked like a small children's doll, only it had specks of brown and red covering it. She couldn't see his face, but she could feel the rage that was overtaking Sebastian. He jumped up on the camel and kicked it in its side, forcing it to run forward towards the city. Before Ashleigh could really react, John was quickly following him towards the city, with Ashleigh trying her best to stay close.

"Sebastian!" John yelled as they ran towards the city. "You must calm down! Running head first into a raging mass of chaos will do us no good to stop Aamon. We need a proper plan of attack!" Sebastian didn't hear him. He didn't hear anything. All he seemed to hear were the screams coming from the city. As John continued to yell at Sebastian to stop, all Ashleigh could do was watch the city continue to smoke, fires becoming visible as they close in. Finally, as they grew closer, Ashleigh had had enough. "Sebastian stop!" she screamed. Sebastian came to a halt, the camel coming within feet of the city entrance. John slowed to a crawl, giving Ashleigh chance to catch up. "Ashleigh," John said giving her a concerned look. "Maybe I should talk to him..." Before he could finish, Ashleigh placed her hand in the air, letting him know to stop. "I understand you two have an unspoken trust, even if you claim to hate his insides for whatever reason," she said. "But I need to talk to him. And he needs to hear it just as much as I need to say it." John backed his camel up, giving her way to stand next to Sebastian. The two stood in silence for a moment, the only real noise coming from the fires crackling in the city. "Ashleigh", Sebastian began. "You don't understand..." "Don't you dare say those words you ginger haired idiot," Ashleigh said, just before covering her mouth. While John covered his mouth, Sebastian simply kept his head down.

"You need to get your head out of the dirt and start thinking clearly for a change. I understand full well that you're having a hard time in all of this, and the view of this city in such disarray is making it worse. But that is no excuse for you to go running in there like a raging bull and risking you're life, as well as everyone else's around you." She looked back at John who, instead of pitching in with his own words, simply nodded his head and urged her to continue. "And I understand that this is a difficult scenario that I might not fully grasp, and that John may be the only other person who truly knows how you're feeling right now," she continued. "But I need you to realize that you can't just act like it's only you and his suggestive voice in all this." She nudged herself closer to him, their camels bumping one another. She placed her hand on his shoulder, to which he finally looked up. To her surprise, He actually had a tear rolling down his cheek. "That damn fool," he said as he wiped his face. "If he had just listened to us, we could have gotten here sooner and none of this would have happened. We could have stopped this from getting as bad as it did." He looked back down at the back of his camel, his hands clenching into fists. "I could have stopped this from happening. No one deserves this kind of pain."

Ashleigh didn't know what to say. She had never seen Sebastian this broken, almost as if he had to watch his own parents pass away in front of him, unable to do anything to help them. Ashleigh went to continue her statement, only to be cut short by John. "You need to stop feeling sorry for yourself you ginger tomato haired fool." He pulled his camel alongside Sebastian's. "As much as I hate to admit it, and believe me I do. But

Maxwell will do anything to make you feel like a rat covered in horse manure. And even I can't stand aside as he treats the threat of Aamon like it isn't even a problem. Which is why I followed you and Ashleigh to your boat and came with you. Because you know how dangerous this is, no matter who says otherwise." Before he could continue any further, another scream broke out in the air, followed by a new billow of smoke. "Now as much as I'd like to continue reassuring you that you are not in fact a waste of space, we should really get going." With that John continued forward, prompting Ashleigh and Sebastian to slowly follow behind him. "Are you alright?" Ashleigh asked. Sebastian kept looking at the back of his camel for a moment, and then wiped his face in his jacket sleeve. "Yes Ashleigh. I'm... I'm fine now. Let's get this done and over with." He flicked the reigns on his camel, prompting it to speed up to John. "And Ashleigh," he said. "It isn't just John and I in this. I know you're here and I do know you can help. But there are things that you cannot know... not yet anyway. "Just please. Give me the time and I will be ready." It had almost become routine at this point. Sebastian has a moment of rage and uncontrolled emotions about his past, he apologizes for not being open right away about the matter, and promises to at some point tell her the truth. And as always, she agreed to wait for him when he was ready. But as they closed in on the entrance to the city, she couldn't help but feel like she wasn't going to get anything more than promises. Promises that wouldn't be kept for some time.

When they entered the city it was much different from the last time they were there. Where there were once merchant stalls were now piles of rubble and ash. Beautiful paintings of the city's prominent religious figures were now covered with black paintings of Aamon. People who she remembered seeing walking around the city and enjoying themselves were now running across the streets in fear, some even huddled on the ground shaking. One man even came up to her camel and began muttering strange words she didn't understand. All she could make out was a reoccurring word. Tayvl. The man continued to say it over and over, sounding as if he was about to die and didn't want to let the word be forgotten. When she finally managed to leave him behind, she asked Sebastian and asked what the word meant. "It means Demon," he said. "These people are fearing for their lives they don't even know what's hurting them really. All they do know is that it's a demon and that it wants nothing but harm to come to these people." Ashleigh looked back at the man she left behind, only to see he was staring at her, scratching his head and moving his mouth in a shaky manner. Looking at his mouth all she could here was that word over and over again. Tayvl. She chose to look away, afraid of what else she might see behind her.

"Sebastian," John said, looking back and forth at the various buildings around him. "You never did say where Aamon was when you found him. How will we know?" Suddenly, the sound of shattered glass came echoing from the group's right. They hurried towards the sound and came to their destination. It was a tall cathedral like building, its walls once white were now stained back with soot. Ashleigh looked up to see what was once a large window but was now an empty hole in the building. Sebastian jumped down from his camel and was met with the sound of crunching glass. He looked down to see chunks of shattered glass, all different colors. When looking up at the window, it became apparent that the window was once intended to show the image of Jesus. In its place now however, was a hole of black emptiness.

"Does this answer your question John?" Sebastian asked, turning back to give him a smirk which obviously hid a look of grimace and worry. John forced a laugh and stepped down from his camel, with Ashleigh doing the same. As they walked towards the cathedral it became apparent that all along the walls of the cathedral, hidden by the markings of red and brown, were words. Most were incoherent and made no sense to Ashleigh, but others look familiar. She saw many different symbols, all of which she couldn't understand. When they finally reached the door, there were two phrases written in brown on the door. "What do they say?" Ashleigh asked. Sebastian walked up and placed his hand on the door, reading the words. *"Arayn aun ir vet aumkumen* and *Der shtn lebn do."* Sebastian said aloud. He pulled his hands off the door and it came with red liquid. "And that means what?" Ashleigh continued. Sebastian reached into his bag and pulled out his canteen, pouring some water onto his hand. "Do you really want to know what it says, or do you want the ruff translation?" Before she could answer, John walked forward and opened the door, creating a loud creaking sound. "Don't baby the girl," he said turning back to face the two. "They're warnings. The first means, 'Enter and you will perish', the second says 'Devil lives here.'" Ashleigh tightened her grip on Sebastian's arm as they led the way into the Cathedral. It was barely visible inside the cathedral, with most the light coming from the shattered window and the open door. As they walked they came across more words and markings, just like the ones that lined the outer walls of the building. "Sebastian…" Ashleigh said as her eyes darted all around her. "I know Ashleigh," Sebastian said. "He's here."

Suddenly, the door behind them slammed shut and a cold gust of wind flew into them. It should have felt refreshing since they had been in all of this heat, but instead it felt harmful and unwelcoming. "Didn't I warn you last time Crusader?" a voice said. Before they could react, an unknown force the group on their knees. "Honestly I tried to be kind to you poor souls, but you simply did not listen." Ashleigh could hear footsteps after a moment, but something didn't seem right about each step. It sounded less like someone's shoe hitting the ground and more like someone dropping a bucket on the ground. As the steps came closer, Ashleigh's uneasiness grew worse. Finally, Aamon came from the shadows, revealing himself. Only he wasn't the same demon that Ashleigh remembered.

He no longer wore the black robes it wore before, donning instead a black loincloth accented with golden stripes. His body itself was tall and muscular, with equally as golden marking all across his body; its horn had grown much larger, with swirling designs leading to the tip of each horn. He even had a mouth, which curved into a sickly grin. The only thing that hadn't changed were his disgusting eyes.

He walked towards the three, focusing mainly on Ashleigh. He leaned down and grabbed her chin, turning her head to see the part of her neck he had

scratched during their first encounter. "It seems you've healed," he said. He let go of her, moving onward towards John. "Now I did not have the pleasure of meeting you before now did I?" he said as he began studying John. "You seem to have a different air about you. I take it you are with the Church?" John simply nodded his head. "Silent. I can respect that." He finally turned to face Sebastian. "Ah the ringleader. I honestly cannot help but enjoy the thought of killing you. Of course, your partner here did insult me," he gestured towards Ashleigh. "But I have no real quarrel with her truthfully. You however..." he snatched Sebastian by his neck, lifting him in the air. Ashleigh wanted to scream at the demon, but her voice wouldn't work. Whether it was fear or Aamon, something was forcing her to remain silent. "You lied to me. You knew damn well what was here and you played the fool." Sebastian's eyes got wide and he began struggling against his grip. "I knew the moment you entered this building who you were and why you were here. You knew the priest who released me, and you were going to help him seal me away. And you managed to play the utmost fool to your peers didn't you?" Sebastian remained silent, forcing his hands onto Aamon's wrist. "What do you have to say for yourself boy? Lying in front of those around you, as well as in front of me and your God. What do you have to say?"

He loosened his grip on Sebastian's neck, allowing air to pass into his lungs. He took a deep breath in, releasing it right into Aamon's face. "My God do you ever shut up?" Aamon's face changed from a grin into a look of utter disbelief. "I beg your pardon?" he asked. "I said, do you ever shut up? If you had actually gotten quiet for a good second or two I would have said that while I did know the priest who came here, I did not know it was you who had taken his place. He sent me a letter some time ago saying he needed help with something and so I came here." He looked down at Ashleigh. "Sorry I lied. I guess now is a good time as any to be honest." He turned his gaze back to Aamon. "And second..." He pulled both his hands off of Aamon's arm. "Don't ever grab Ashleigh like that ever again."

Suddenly, John jumped up and thrust his blade at Aamon. He dropped Sebastian to the ground, just missing the blade, but he wasn't fast enough. The blade grazed his left arm, causing it to pour black liquid and steam. He hissed at John, his eyes turning to slit irises. "How did you break free of my control?" John stretched his arm, motioning the sword towards Aamon. It only took me a few second to break free of your grip. All it took then was a matter of waiting for the right moment to strike. Ashleigh could control her body again, so she rushed to help Sebastian up from the ground. "Are you ok?" she asked. Sebastian looked up at her while he rubbed his throat. "For now, yes. Are you?" Ashleigh nodded her head, lifting him from the ground. Before they could continue, John quickly punched Sebastian in the arm. "You mean to tell me you've known who let him out this whole time and you didn't even bother to tell us?" John exclaimed. "Why wouldn't you have told us this earlier?" Sebastian rubbed his arm. "Is this really the time or place to be getting mad at me when we should be focusing on that?" Sebastian responded as he pointed over to Aamon. Only Aamon wasn't where he once was. In his place was a simmering pool of black liquid. "Where did he go?" Ashleigh asked. She was cut off by what could only be described as a knife scraping against stone. She could only guess it was Aamon wailing in pain. "That blade..." Aamon said. He jumped out of the shadows, leaping towards John. He swung his sword in an arc, just nicking Aamon's ankle. He fell to the ground, clutching his leg. The three inched their way close to him, with John in the lead and holding his word outward. It forced Aamon to back up against a wall.

"Why..." he stammered. "It's made from melted silver and it was quenched in a vat of holy water," John said, answering before he even got a chance to ask. "This sword was made to kill demons like you, and it will make good work of you if you do not tell us where the priest who summoned you is? We know you need him alive, otherwise you'd be in your true form by now." Ashleigh peeked out from behind Sebastian. "So that isn't his true form?" she asked. "No..." Aamon stammered. "If it was, you three would be dead where you stand. And as for the priest..."

Aamon lifted one of his blood-soaked hands and snapped his fingers. And without warning, a large flame came to life at the back of the cathedral. Its blinded Ashleigh, filling the room with an orange light. It almost felt like the light of the fire began fighting with the light from the shattered window, each taking up a portion of the room. When her eyes finally adjusted, Ashleigh looked to the flame and saw that in front of it, stood a large wooden cross. And on that cross, hung an old man covered in scars. Without warning, Sebastian began running to the old man. But before he could get very far, a shadow beneath his feet lifted from the floor and turned into a large claw, grabbing Sebastian by the leg and pulling him back. Ashleigh went to warn John, but she was too late. The arm swung Sebastian under John's feet, causing him to fall and drop the sword. Aamon saw his chance and took it, rushing after John and Sebastian. He lifted them both off the ground and pushed them into a wall. She quickly dodged John's sword as it fell to the ground, just missing its blade. As she stood up, she saw Sebastian and John struggling against the demon's grip. Without thinking, she quickly grabbed the sword and ran for the old man by the fire. She cut the man down, his body falling to the floor. She dropped the sword and checked to see he was breathing, and was relieved to see that he was, in fact, alive. She shook the man awake, trying to gain his attention. After a brief moment, he came to and focused on her.

"Sir, listen," she began. "You don't know me, but you obviously know my companions. We need to stop Aamon. I know you're the one who let him out and I know you have some good reason as to why, I hope. But tell me. What do I do to stop him?" The man simply stared at her. He looked between her and the now enraged Aamon, who was close to choking Sebastian and John unconscious. She grabbed his face, forcing him to look her in the eyes. "Sir! What do we do?" The man didn't know what the young girl in front of him was saying, but the look in her eyes told him enough. He looked behind her at the sword she used to cut him down, and simply pointed to it. Ashleigh quickly grabbed it and handed it to him, prompting him to take it. As he held it, he reached into a pocket in his pants and pulled out a small vial. It had a dark silver liquid inside it. He prompted Ashleigh to open the jar. After she opened the vial, she handed it back to him, to which he began pouring the liquid along the edge of the sword.

After he emptied the contents of the bottle, he gently set it aside. Then, he handed her the sword. "Wait, you mean me?" Ashleigh stammered. "I can't use this I've never swung anything larger than a kitchen knife I can't I..." The old man didn't let her finish. All he did was gently take her left hand and place it onto the handle of the sword. He then looked her in the eyes and let go. Before she could say anything else, his body went limp and he fell onto his back. With tears in her eyes, Ashleigh stood up and held the blade up high. The handle felt uncomfortable, but she didn't care. She wasn't going to watch any more suffering.

She turned to face Aamon who, at this point, had dropped Sebastian and John onto the ground. She could see they were still breathing, which relieved Ashleigh. "Well that was exciting," he said, rubbing his wrist. He walked with a faint limp, caused by the cut on his ankle. "But I think it's time we ended this. With another snap of his fingers the fire behind Ashleigh exploded into a violent red color. The fire began to spread across the building, lighting everything ablaze. And as it did so, she could not help but hear a faint noise. It was dismissible at first, but if you focus hard enough... "You hear them don't you?" Aamon asked. Her thought was interrupted by Aamon smiling. "The screams. Most do not catch it right away and I'm impressed you did so quickly. Those are the screams of Hell itself. The change of color in the flames is to represent the blood that flows through their bodies and into the underworld. This is what will overtake this city. And it will signal his coming." He threw his arms into the air, as if praising the raging fire. "He will come in due time!" he yelled. "Even now I can feel his presence! Witness girl, as a fallen angel comes home!" Ashleigh gripped the handle of the blade, her knuckles turning white. "I could honestly give less of a damn about what you're talking about right now," she said, tears running down her cheeks. "Just do me a kind favor and get the hell out of here." She rushed at Aamon, readying the blade for one large swing.

"You wish to strike me?" Aamon jokingly asked. "Very Well, I will give you one chance. Even with that sword, there is nothing in this cathedral that could kill me whilst I stand next to this raging fire." HE held open his arms and closed his eyes, cockily waiting for Ashleigh She ran as fast as she could, preparing to swing the sword. As she was within feet of Aamon, he opened his eyes and smiled at the young girl. But his smile quickly changed as she got closer. The closer he looked, the more he realized that on the blade, was a dark liquid. A liquid that he knew could do terrible things. "Before he could think, act, or even say anything, Ashleigh swung the blade at Aamon's neck. And with a following *plop*, the fire slowly died. Ashleigh stood still, afraid to move or even think. All she could do, was hold a sword and stand next to a headless demon.

After a moment of silence, Sebastian came to. He looked around the building, which was now covered in scorch marks and ash, unsure of what actually happened. And then he saw Ashleigh standing there, holding a sword next to a still standing Aamon. He rushed to her side, taking the sword from her and dropping it to the ground. "Ashleigh," Sebastian said. He shook her shoulders, urging her to answer. "Ashleigh please talk to me. Ashleigh!" She shook her head. Her face was covered in sweat and tears, her eyes puffy and red. Without saying anything, she gripped Sebastian in a hug. She began crying into his coat, her sobbing making the only sound in the cathedral. All Sebastian could think to do was place his hand on her head and hold it there. It seemed to help as her crying slowly stopped. "Is it over?" she asked. "Yes," Sebastian said. "It's over. I promise." Ashleigh looked at Sebastian with a soaked red face. "The old man..." she said pointing to the now scorched cross. "He... he didn't make it. He told me what to do and..." Sebastian put his hand ton her mouth, urging her to not worry about it. "I figured as much. With what he had already been through, I didn't expect him to live as long as he did." He looked back to the old man's body, which had gotten caught in the fire. "I just wish I could've apologized for not coming sooner." "Who was he?" she asked. Sebastian looked at the ground then looked her in the eyes. "He was one of the few people in the church I could have considered a friend. He may have stayed with the church, but the hatred everyone else feels towards me never changed how he felt about me. He was... he was a good man." Sebastian shook his head, letting the memories pass by. "But it's over. Whatever Aamon was planning you stopped it. You." He wiped one of her tears, which made her smile.

Their moment of bonding was interrupted by John groaning. "Tell me Sebastian," he began. He slowly stood up from the floor, rubbing his throat. "How the hell did you manage to find her? She's done more work in a weeks' time than you've managed to do in how many years?" The comment made Ashleigh laugh, and it caused Sebastian to scowl at John. As he came over, Ashleigh couldn't help but look at the still standing body of Aamon. "I don't understand," she said, studying the corpse. "What actually killed him? He said it himself, there wasn't anything here that could kill him. So, what did it?" John walked over to the Aamon's body picked up his sword, noticing what was left of the silver liquid. "I believe it was this," he said. He showed the sword to Sebastian, who in turn studied it. "What was it he poured on there?" Ashleigh asked. As he looked at it, Sebastian wiped his finger against the blade, picking some liquid with it. "It's a mixture of Aamon's blood with holy water and bits of silver. This is an uncommon concoction used to banish demons in an exorcism, mixing the demons blood with various holy elements. He must have been hiding it and Aamon never knew. And if Aamon hadn't let his own hubris get the best of him, he might have actually survived." He handed the blade back to John. "Good thing that didn't happen though," Sebastian said jokingly. Ashleigh looked at the body one last time, picking up a stick and poking it in the chest. "So, is he dead then?" she asked. Sebastian shook his head, causing her to worry one more. "Demons can be killed yes, but only for so long. And if they are powerful enough, they won't die at all they'll just get sent back to the Inferno from where they came from." Sebastian took Ashleigh's stick and poked Aamon's body hard enough to knock it over, causing it to make thud on the wood floor. "And I don't think he'll be coming back any time soon."

Chapter 9

The three waked out of the old cathedral and were met with the remaining citizens of the city. They walked slowly towards them; some being carried by others. They all looked between the group and the building, as if waiting for something to happen. Ashleigh went to ask Sebastian what they were waiting for, but she didn't get the chance. A young girl with a small doll came up to them. She had skin like the sand and wore tattered white robes. As Ashleigh looked closer, she saw that the doll she held was the same one that Sebastian had picked up on their way into the city. Without warning, the little girl grabbed her hand and pulled her down to be eye level with her. Ashleigh locked eyes with the girl, unable to look away from her startlingly silver eyes. "Hat der farzeenish geyn avek?" the little girl asked. Unsure of what to say, Ashleigh looked back at Sebastian. "What did she say just now?" she asked, sweat dripping down her forehead. "She said... did the monster go away," he replied. Ashleigh looked back at the girl, then back at Sebastian. "Well what do I tell her?" she asked again, getting agitated. Sebastian stood quiet for a moment, and then leaned forward to Ashleigh ear and whispered something. All the while the little girl stood in silence, waiting for her answer. Ashleigh turned around, looking the young girl in the eyes and said, "Di farzeenish vet nit zeyn kumen tsurik tomid vider." The little girl then smiled, hugging Ashleigh as tight as possible, and then walked away towards a woman who looked no older than Ashleigh herself. The two made eye contact for a moment, and then the woman smiled, nodding her head in thanks.

"Well isn't this sweet," a familiar voice said. The peaceful moment was interrupted by Maxwell who, appearing from nowhere, had a small group of priests with him. Ashleigh recognized many faces from her visit to the Church, and for a brief moment, felt a tinge of fear as to the idea of whether or not Constantine or his cronies were among them. The crowd separated from one another, creating a path for the group to walk through. The group finally stopped in the center of the crowd. All except for Maxwell who walked up to the three, followed by a slender man with long black hair. He had what looked like a journal similar to Sebastian's, only this one was black with no cross. "My fellow worshippers of God," Maxwell said, turning to face the crowd. "You have been saved. My disciples have done their duty in the name of the lord and saved you from this wretched evil that plagued your holy land." As he spoke, the man next to him spoke after he did, repeating every word in the language of the villagers. "We are speakers of his word and we have come to offer you sanctity and care. We beseech you to come with us, and you will be cared for." He looked down at the ground, noticing a small snake. Before it could react, he quickly stepped on its body and pinned it to the ground. He leaned down to pick it up, easing his hand under its writhing head. It snapped back and forth at his hand, even biting it once or twice, but he didn't seem to notice. When he had a firm grip under its head, he placed his thumb under its chin, and quickly crushed the snake's neck under his thumb. The snake stopped moving so suddenly, it almost seemed unnatural for anyone to snap an animal's neck so precisely. "Behold! I have killed his symbol swiftly and I am unharmed. Please, come with us, and you too will remain unharmed."

Everyone around them seemed to be enthralled by Maxwell and his tricks, swarming him without warning. He placed the snake in a bag he had hanging over his shoulder, and with a wave of his hand he had his men separate him from the crowd. "Now, back to business," he said, his eccentric smile replaced with a sickly grin. "Where is Aamon's body? It can't be so easily disposed of, so we shall take it to the Basilica to be cleansed and burned." Before Ashleigh could make any comment towards what he just did in front of the crowd, Sebastian stepped forward. "It's in the cathedral laying on the ground. The head is there too so don't forget to grab that while you're in there." Ashleigh wanted to cut in, but she could tell it wasn't the time. Without any other remarks or even bodily movements, she could see that Sebastian was doing everything in his power to not deck Maxwell in his mouth. "Good," the old man said. "And what about the priest who let Aamon out to begin with? He will surely pay for what he's done." John cut into the conversation, replying for Sebastian. "He's already dead. We found him dead before we had arrived. He left some tools that aided us in Aamon's execution, but that was it. I will see to his body's disposal sir." Ashleigh was dumbfounded, surprised that he would so quickly cover up the original death of the man who helped them. Maxwell placed his hand on his chin, contemplating the idea. "Alright then. It's settled. We will see you at the Basilica in due time John." Maxwell began to walk away only to stop just as fast as he started.

"Oh, and Sebastian." He turned around and placed his hand on Sebastian's shoulder, pulling the two of them closer to one another. "Thank you for being so cooperative. We wouldn't want these kind people to see you assaulting their true savior. I mean after all it would mark a second city you aren't allowed to enter, and I'm certain you don't want that. Do you?" Sebastian stood there, silent as can be. "Yes sir," he replied quietly. "Hmm? I didn't quite catch that. Do speak up my boy." Sebastian sighed. "I said, yes sir." "Maxwell smiled, and then walked off into the distance. After a moment, two men walked out of the cathedral, dragging two large sacks behind them. Ashleigh could see Aamon's horns poking through the sack, and it made her sick thinking about it. He two men placed the corpse on the back of a camel, hanging the head around its neck. And with that the group left the city of the Son, its people in awe of the mysterious man of God who claimed to be their savior. Ashleigh wanted to say so many things in that moment. She wanted to kick and scream, she wanted to call Maxwell so many harsh and cruel names. But in those thoughts, a phrase Eren used to tell her came to mind.

"With every violent act or phrase, you do or say to another person, you give them fuel to keep making you feel this way. Sometimes in the darkest of moments, the best thing you can do is ignore them, telling yourself that you yourself are the stronger person. It's better than punching someone's teeth in that's for sure."

Ashleigh decided to save her emotions for when the time was right. And for now, all she could do was to keep Sebastian from acting out before she does.

As the group led by Maxwell walked off towards their destination, Maxwell looked to the man with long black hair for certainty. "Are we out of their sight Francesco?" Maxwell asked. "Yes, my liege," the man replied, nodding his head. "Good. We can continue then." He urged the camel with Aamon's corpse closer to his own camel, pulling the string that kept it closed. He pulled out the small snake from earlier and slipped it headfirst into the sacks opening. As expected, the snake slithered into the sack. After a moment, it began to writhe and shake, continuing for a few second until finally, it stopped entirely. Maxwell raised his hand, forcing the group to stop. He pointed at one priest to remove the sack from the camel and open it. The priest complied with his master, not questioning as he was told. As he placed it down on the ground, he didn't even get a chance to open the sack itself, as a clawed hand shot out and grabbed his face. The priest panicked, tearing at the sickly arm that clenched his face. As it kept its grasp, the man's body began to sink inward, as if his organs were being sucked right out of his body through the hand. It continued until all that was left of the man was nothing but a grey husk in black robes. His body fell to the ground, and the claw pulled itself back into the bag. Then, a single claw tore through the fabric, tearing it open. Out of the torn sack rose a naked figure who had not been there before. He had a frail and sunken body, the right side a lighter skin tone, and the left being a strange purple color, almost as if it were a still dying body. He had long white hair that looked the color of fresh bone.

"Well?" Maxwell asked. "Are you fed?" The stranger's eyes opened, revealing black eyes with slit red irises. "*Dove Sono*?" the stranger asked in a low raspy voice. "You're in a desert just outside the City of the Son. We used Aamon as a distraction to resurrect you. You won't quite remember everything my lord, but in due time, it will come to you." The figure stood there for another moment, one of Maxwell's men handing him a fresh cloak and loincloth. "Sir," Francesco said, trying for Maxwell's attention. "Is this truly our master?" He looks different from how the scriptures depicted him." Maxwell didn't turn to face Francesco, as all he could do was stare at the figure. "They never are what we expect them to be," Maxwell replied. "Now hurry, get the other sack and place the body inside it. We cannot arrive to the Basilica empty handed now can we?" With that Francesco stuffed the dead priest's body into the fresh sack and threw it over his camel. After dressing himself, the figure placed the cloak over his shoulders and pulled the hood over his head. Maxwell noticed under his hair were two tattoos on his back; a pair of angel wings, one white and beautiful, the other dark and tattered. The man climbed unto his camel, and the party continued forward. Maxwell kept close to the stranger, making sure he never left his sight. "Do you remember, my liege?" The man looked down at his left hand, flexing his fingers and studying the long black claws. *"Si'. Sta venendo verso di me lentamente, ma sta arrivando."* "Good," Maxwell replied. "It will take some time, but we will restore you to your full abilities. And then we shall begin our plan."

Maxwell sat in silence, waiting for a response that had yet to come. "Are you alright my liege?" he asked. The man kept flexing his hand, even proceeding to drag his nail along the neck of the camel, drawing a line of blood from the creature. *"E ' passato molto tempo dall'ultima volta che ho camminato al fianco di uomini mortali. Non sono abituato ad avere un corpo come questo."* "I understand my liege, it will take some getting used to having a body like this again. But it will all be worth it in due time. In the meantime, why not give this new body a new name? A name to be remembered throughout the ages by all who hear it." The man set his hand down on the reigns and looked out at the setting sun in the distance. Something about it seemed both peaceful and powerful to the man. It reminded him of the many depictions God had laid down upon the world, a man with red skin and horns, a forked tongue and all. *"I mortali della vostra Chiesa hanno una lingua piuttosto bella. La tua parola per chi sono e ' cio ' che mi chiameranno. Diavolo."* Maxwell looked at him both intrigued and impressed. "Alright then, Diavolo, we will make your name more known than God himself." Diavolo looked up at the sky, pondering the thought of how *'He'* must be feeling right now, "That will be a good day Maxwell," he said. "That will be a good day."

Part IV

The Truth

Chapter 1

It had been a few months since the incident in Eretz, and Sebastian was not the same. After Maxwell and his associates left the city, the citizens clawing at their heels for approval, Sebastian and John proceeded to help with the cleanup of the city. Everyone seemed to have ignored what they had done for them, thinking to themselves that it was all in Maxwell's words their safety had arrived. And even though he said nothing, choosing to focus on keeping a smile and helping the victims of Aamon's wrath, he was deeply troubled. His eyes didn't have their usual glow about them, being replaced by a sad and pale haze.

After a few weeks, the city was in well enough shape that they would be fine on their own. The group returned to a port side colony they had arrived in, meeting up with Clyde. Despite Sebastian's constant offers to return John to the Basilica, he refused and stated that it'd be better if Sebastian take some time away from going too close to the country; that and he had some personal business to attend to with an, "old friend". With that he took a separate boat to the Basilica. After he left Sebastian didn't say much. All he did say was that their next stop was a portside town in England, which then they'll take a large ocean vessel to the Americas. When asked why all Sebastian would say is that he needs to see someone in the West for some medicinal needs, and that was all. The first boat ride was silent, filled with occasional chatter about the passing schools of fish or how drunk Clyde was when they found him in Ostia. It took a month or so to reach England, and on the day of their arrival it seemed almost like a warning of events to come.

Sebastian described where they were going to be arriving was a poor city, where people would be fighting cats and dogs for their next meal. Ashleigh laughed it off, claiming it couldn't have been that bad, but Sebastian got a sudden look in his eyes, proceeding to say that it was just as bad, if not worse than how he described it. "We won't be there long," he would tell her. "Just long enough to reach the boat we need and then go from there." All she felt she could do was shake her head and nod in agreement. She wanted to console him after everything that's happened, but he just seemed too distant from her. As if having to deal with Maxwell, and now this city, had somehow built a wall that she needed to cross over. But it was proving more and more difficult with every attempt.

When they first arrived, it seemed well enough. They arrived in a city Sebastian referred to as Bristol, and he stated that while they could just leave from there, they would need to part ways with Clyde and continue on their own to London, a city Ashleigh had heard of in her time at the tavern, though it mainly came from travelers from England boasting about the recent construction of their large clock tower, claiming it to be one of the greatest feats of human ingenuity for years to come. While the boasting did get old very fast, she couldn't help but marvel at the grandness of the clock tower now that she could see it with her own eyes. The sheer height of it, as well as the determination the city had to build something new after that horrible fire.

"It's impressive isn't it?" Sebastian asked. She was so lost in thought that she didn't even realize that she had been standing there in the middle of a large crowd of people. He stood there watching her, a hint of a smile sneaking its way across his face. "I suppose it is," Ashleigh said, bringing herself back to reality. "What's more impressive is that's the first smile you've had since we left the city..." Ashleigh caught herself as she spoke, not having considered what she had to say. "Sebastian I'm sorry I..." she tried to apologize but was cut off by Sebastian placing his hand on her shoulder. "You're quite alright Ashleigh," he said. She looked into his eyes, seeing a small hint of that bright familiar glow. "I had a hard time I must admit that," he continued. "And I won't recover so easily. What happened there was... unpleasant." He shuddered at the thought, his eyes turning pale. "But what happened has happened, and we shouldn't dwell on it for too long. Once we get to the Americas we should be set from there." He continued walking, forcing Ashleigh to rush after him. "On that note," she began. "Who is it we're going to see out there? You never did actually tell me." Sebastian kept his eyes forward, determined to reach the port. "An old friend of mine," he said as he adjusted his glasses. "I've known him for some time, and I got to him in case of any emergencies that arise. Be it medicinal or Supernatural." Ashleigh nodded her head, choosing to stay quiet from then on. She was running out of ideas for small talk, and this was the most Sebastian has said in almost two months, and she was worried she wouldn't get any other chances to talk to him before he closed himself off. Just before she could call out his name, he threw his arms into the air in forced joy. "Here we are," he said. "This is the ship that will take us to the Americas." Ashleigh caught up to him and was shocked at what she saw.

The ship was massive, almost as large as an entire block of her village. It had three large sails, each as wide as the ship itself. On the side it had the name "The Mayweather". "This is the ship that's going to take us to the Americas?" Ashleigh asked. "Yes," Sebastian said. "This is an immigration vessel used by travelers of this country to make way to other lands. It's also used for transporting goods to other lands." Sebastian looked up at the large ship, studying it. "Ironic isn't it? This ship used to help people migrate to a country that itself is home to men and women alike who pledged to escape this very country we stand on. It was only a couple hundred years ago that the English Colonists embarked on a journey to find their own land, and now here we are. Two hundred years later and embarking to that very country." Ashleigh looked at him amazed. "You know a surprising bit about the history here. How much did the Basilica teach you?" He shook his head thinking back to his younger days. "Well it was common practice to understand the basic history of the various countries we may visit. And besides it's easy to now these things when you've..." He grew silent, losing his nerve. "When you've... what? When you've what Sebastian?" Ashleigh shook his shoulder snapping him out of his trance. "It's nothing," he said abruptly, moving his arm away. "Really it's nothing. Let's just get to the ship. It should be leaving soon, and we wouldn't want to miss it." He continued walking, urging Ashleigh to follow.

When they arrived at the ship, there was a crowd of people all crowding a small bridge that led up to the deck of the ship. While people yelled and cried, two men ran a small table, two stacks of paper standing next to them. They wore black uniforms and had hats that looked like strangely shaped eggs. One man tried to speak to the person closest to the table, while the other urged people to calm down and stay under control, occasionally swinging a small black stick. Sebastian grabbed Ashleigh's hand and pulled her through the crowd, weaving through the mass of people. People began giving him dirty looks and even tried to shove him back behind them, to which there was no success. "Are you sure this is ok Sebastian?" Ashleigh asked. "Don't you think this is rather rude what we're doing to these people?" Sebastian didn't look back to respond, simply trying to make a path through the crowd. "If we wait behind them Ashleigh we'll never get on that boat." He politely moved a group of men out of the way, getting closer to the front. "You saw the city. It's a nightmare to be in and everyone in their right mind is doing what they can to survive. Be it trying to get on this boat or surviving naturally. And if I'm being frank, I wouldn't blame them if they wanted to leave."

By the time they reached the front the men had just finished ushering a couple and a child up the bridge. "That's all folk's," the man with the stick yelled. "There's no more room on the boat, so please leave calmly and orderly. It will return in four to five months' time, to which you can all try to get on once again." People began leaving, murmuring under their breaths some rather harsh words, most of which were focused towards the two men. "Excuse me my good sirs!" Sebastian yelled. The men began taking down the bridge, until Sebastian placed his hand on one man's shoulder. "Please my good gentlemen, we need to get on that ship." The man looked up at him, his eyes cold and tired. "Sorry mate no can do," he said. "That's all we can fit right now. Besides even if we wanted to, we have no more forms for you to fil out." Sebastian began talking with his hands, trying his best to keep them from taking down the bridge. "Surely you can make an acceptation for a preacher of God," he said, trying to see if his "title" might help them. "I told you no exceptions. Not even for a man of God." Sebastian began rambling, trying to do or say anything that might sway their minds.

As he spoke, Ashleigh looked up and saw the couple that had went before them. It was a young couple with a small newborn infant. Ashleigh looked at the couple, seeing that the two were in terrible shape. The woman was pale, her skin white and her hair matted brown. The man was just as pale, his cheeks sunken and his body wiry. Ashleigh locked eyes with the woman. For as pale as she was, seemed lively and full of focus. She then looked to see Sebastian arguing with the men, one even preparing to pull out his stick. The woman looked to the man, pulling on his coat. They spoke a few words, ending with the man smiling and nodding his head. The man began leading the woman down the bridge. The sudden movement got the men's attention, taking him away from Sebastian's ramblings. "Ma'am, you shouldn't be coming back down," he said placing the stick away. "The boat will be leaving soon." The woman ignored him, continuing to walk. The man went to stop her, but she raised her hand to silence him. "I understand the boat is leaving soon," the woman said. "Which is why I am choosing to stay and let these travelers take our place." She reached the end, taking a step off the bridge and onto the dock. Now that Ashleigh could see her closely, she saw that the woman was very unwell. She was beaded with sweat, looking ready to pass out; her limbs were frail, barely able to hold her body upright. The man was just as bad, his chest just as much sunken and his body sweating as badly as hers.

The woman took a few steps towards Ashleigh and began studying her. Ashleigh looked her in the eyes, seeing a determined focus, but didn't understand what it meant. She kept studying her and then looked over at Sebastian. She looked him up and down, and then turned to the man behind her. "You are ok with this?" she asked him. The man silently smiled and nodded his head in acknowledgement. "We will give you two our place on the ship. I think you will need it more than I will." Ashleigh didn't know what to say, but Sebastian did it for it. "No ma'am we couldn't possibly force you to do that. It's alright we can try to find another ship there's really no need..." The woman lifted her hand once more, forcing him to be silent. "If it were that simple you wouldn't have tried so hard to sway these men's judgements." The men sat in silence, watching the encounter unfold. "And besides, our bodies wouldn't make the journey. We would most likely make it the first month and then..." The woman grew silent, the man placing his hand on her shoulder. "I just have one small task to ask of you two." The woman adjusted her baby and motioned it towards Ashleigh. Ashleigh knew what was happening and was unsure of what to say or do. She wanted to tell her no, to tell her that there was no way they would be able to care for the child. But the woman had a determined look in her eyes. "I'm sorry ma'am but we can't possibly take the child," Sebastian said, his eyes darting between Ashleigh and the child. "But we aren't even prepared for this sort of thing." "I understand that," she said. "As I said our bodies cannot make the journey. But she can." She placed her hand on the child's head, tussling the infant's thin silvery hair. "She has a future outside of this country. And she shouldn't be held back by us. I'm not asking you to take over as her mother. All I'm asking is that you simply care for her for the journey itself. Where you take her after that is up to you." The woman then placed her hands-on Ashleigh's own hands. She locked her eyes with her own. "But please," she continued. Take care of her. For us."

Ashleigh didn't know what to say. She looked down at the small child and caught its gaze. The little one opened its small eyes to reveal a stunning amber color. It reminded Ashleigh of the morning sunrise in her town. The young girl started to wriggle in Ashleigh's arms, even grabbing a hold of Ashleigh's finger; to feel such a small hand grabbing her finger, it was almost too unreal to her. She had never even held a baby prior to this moment. Her trance was interrupted by Sebastian's hand resting on her shoulder. She looked at him and saw he was beaded with sweat, nervous as he tried to keep the guards from kicking them all off the boat.

"Please ma'am I insist I simply can't ask you to sacrifice your place on the boat for us," he said, trying to end the conversation. "We can find another way I assure you. I don't want to burden you." The woman remained focused, her decision unchanged. "I understand," she said with a smile. "But I'd like to hear what the young lady has to say." Ashleigh looked up to face not only Sebastian, but just as well the woman, her husband, and the two officers. Ashleigh stood in silence, looking between Sebastian and the baby. Sebastian went to say her name, hoping to urge her to turn the baby away, but the woman raised he hand up to silence him. "Let her decide sir," she said sternly. "What do you want young miss?" Ashleigh looked the woman in the eyes, and then took one more look down at the baby. It closed its eyes but still held strong to her finger. Something about holding the baby felt right but shew wasn't sure why. But what she was sure of, was what to do next.

"We can take the baby ma'am," she said smiling at the woman. "This is… very new to me. But I feel like for this journey we can manage." She turned to Sebastian who, begrudgingly nodded his head. "Can't argue when you've set your mind to something I suppose." He looked to the man who had remained silent. "But first, is there any specific food we should give her? And what about when we arrive, I assume you two filed out a form saying who you are. Won't they question us when they see us?" The man began fiddling inside a small bag that hung on his shoulder. "There should be no trouble when you arrive." His voice was shrill and raspy, as if it were rubbed in sand and then had spittoon juices poured down it. He pulled out a small piece of parchment paper and took the bag off his shoulder. "When you arrive just show them this paper. We didn't put our names on it yet so you can put yours instead. What you do after that is up to you. As for feeding her just give her small pieces of bread and small cups of water, no more than enough to fill your palm." He handed Sebastian the bag and then the paper.

He looked it over and folded up into the bag. "Thank you," he said, his concern fading slightly. "But are you sure about this? I mean this is your own child and your entrusting it to two people you just met. And the child is recommended to have the mother's milk to stay healthy. So, if you're in any way unsure..." The woman shook her head. "We are fine with this I promise you. As I said I won't be able to make the journey, and that goes the same for my own resources. I tried feeding her naturally, but it just didn't work out as well, there is also animal milk on the ship you can use if need be. And I believe she is in good hands." She looked over at Ashleigh and smiled. Ashleigh smiled back, adjusting her arms to make the child more comfortable.

"I do hate to end this but are you done here?" one of the officers said. "We have to be there in due time, and we can't wait any longer so we must get going." Suddenly the other man began nudging Ashleigh and Sebastian up the bridge and onto the boat. As they reached the helm they were met with a mass of people, some old some young, some dying more so than the couple. The two men began to undo the knots with the couple watching from the docks. As the boat began to pull away, Sebastian began looking through the bag and found a few spare notes and a small glass bottle with a mouthpiece for the infant. As Ashleigh looked at the baby, she realized that she had no idea what the name of the child was. She quickly rushed to the side of the boat to yell at the couple, but she was too late; the dock was soon too far to yell, and the boat was getting further by the second. Sebastian walked over and asked what was wrong. "I just realized that they never actually told us her name." Sebastian stood silent for a moment, and then quickly reached into the bag. He pulled out the parchment; he unfolded it to look at the names. "Well it says here that her name is... Sybil. Sybil Atkins." Ashleigh looked down at the child. "Sybil Atkins? Yes, I can see it." She wiggled her finger in front of the small child who eagerly reached out and grabbed it.

The next three months were a grueling journey to America. With little to no experience caring for a child, she looked to the other mothers on the ship. They showed her how to feed her properly and even the best means of changing and disposing of her used undergarments. When she was asked about her childcare experience, all she could say was that she only ever watched people care for the young, never taking part herself. After a couple of days, she began to get used to Sybil and he needs, almost becoming routine. Sebastian would pitch in now and again, offering to watch her so Ashleigh could get some rest; she hadn't realized it, but she had been caring for her non-stop with no real rest in between. When he would take her, she would lay down and just feel like she was lying in a cloud.

There were no issues while traveling, only an occasional storm here and there. As they moved Sebastian never seemed to settle; there were times where he wouldn't sleep for what seemed like days, choosing to just watch the ocean pass by. She nearly had to force him to lay down at times just so he didn't fall over the side of the boat. "Sorry Ashleigh," he'd say. "I just can't seem to rest my mind. Restless thoughts I suppose. Restless thoughts…" She always worried about him, never sure what he was really thinking. It seemed the visit to the Basilica sparked something in him. Something old and unpleasant.

When they finally arrived at their destination Ashleigh was amazed by the view she had. "So, this is New York then?" she asked Sebastian as they watched the city come to light from the rising sun behind them. Yes, beautiful isn't it? It's funny how a small group of people were able to escape England and become what they are today." He looked down at the water, almost entranced by how it was moving. "But not all of us get that kind of freedom, do we?" he said in a depressing tone. Ashleigh had finally had enough. "Ok Sebastian," she began. "You need to start talking to me because this is getting really old and I'm getting sick of you making excuses and…" she was cut off by the sound of a bell ringing. She turned around to see the man who held the bell also held a piece of parchment. "Everyone please come forward and make sure you are all accounted for. We can't have any unwanted travelers on the ship, so we need to make sure everyone is who they say they are." Sebastian looked back at Ashleigh, frowning at the sudden turn of events. "We should make sure we have all the necessary information on the paper they gave us in London," he said. "Do you have it on you?" Ashleigh's face grew red, but she begrudgingly pulled out the paper with Sybils name on it. "Don't think I'm going to forget this Sebastian. You better talk to me about all this. And soon." She pulled out the paper and handed it to him. She had written their names and ages on it about a month or so into their journey. She wasn't sure about using her maiden name and since Sebastian never said his full name, she just wrote down that they were Ashleigh And Sebastian Atkins, immigrants from Eastern Europe who wanted a better life.

Sebastian looked it over, making sure everything was as it should be. He at one point asked for a piece of charcoal and he began rewriting something. "You spelt my name wrong you know," he said. Not 'ion' but 'ian'." Ashleigh looked at him flustered, rocking the baby in her arms. "You never exactly showed me your name before, much less how its spelt." He looked at her shocked. "I wrote it down in the journal you should see it every time you open it. "Your handwriting is so hashed it looks like a chicken wrote it. I can barely make it out sometimes. I even had to ask John to clarify certain words for me since he's known you longer." Saying those words jabbed her a little bit more, reminding herself of her current predicament. Sebastian continued his work, distracted from her in her current state. "Well I'm sorry if my handwriting isn't perfect," he said, finishing his name. "I mean yours is no better, of course you do have a hint of cursive so that helps it…"

He finally looked at her and saw how unnerved she was. In some small part of his mind he knew that he wouldn't be able to hide the truth from her much longer. He folded up the paper into his coat and walked over to Ashleigh, placing his hands on her shoulders. "Ashleigh, I'm sorry that I'm being so secretive," he said, trying to get her to look at him. "But you must understand there are things a person is worried about sharing. Especially when your someone like me and…" "But that's just it," he interrupted. "I don't know you. Not fully anyway. Yes, I know who you are on the outside. But I know next to nothing about the rest of you." She gestured for him to take the baby for a moment, to which he agreed; she began pacing on the deck looking out at the city as drew near. "I know that you are British by origin, I know you came from a very questionable church, and I know that whenever I asked about why the church hates you or where you really come from you get hesitant and start covering up the truth with excuses or promises of telling me the truth." She walked back over and looked Sebastian in the eyes, to which he couldn't return the look. "Even now you won't look at me even when I'm just bringing it up. I would trust you with most if not, everything about who I am. Why can't you treat me the same way?" Sebastian had a face that looked like he wanted to say something, but a part of him was holding him back.

And before he could get the chance, the man with the bell had come to them. "You two have your forms?" he asked in a scratchy voice, sounding like he'd been smoking nothing but an old pie these past three months. "Yes, actually we do. Um Ashleigh could you take Sybil for a moment?" She silently nodded her head and took the baby. Strangely enough she didn't cry very much since they had left, the most every having been at night. But for whatever reason, she had remained relatively silent, taking her meals and changings in a rather calm manner.

The man looked over their forms over three times, making sure everything was in order; finally, he folded the papers and handed them back to Sebastian. "Everything appears to be in order," he said. "Just make sure to show those to the men on the docks and they'll get the rest sorted out." "Thank you," Ashleigh said. He then walked off, turning his attention to the next group of people. Sebastian turned around to see that Ashleigh had gone back to the side of the boat, where a group of people had begun to gather. He followed the group and mad his way through, eventually coming back to Ashleigh. "So," Ashleigh said. "What now? We're here in America. Where do we go from here?" He looked out at the incoming docks thinking to their next destination. "Now, we get our American Identification cards, get ourselves a ticket to the Nebraska territories, and we go from there." She looked up at him, Sybil beginning to fuss slightly in her arms. "What's in the Nebraska territories?" she asked. He looked at her and smiled, placing his hand on the child's head. "The Cheyenne Indians Ashleigh. That's what's out there.

Chapter 2

Ashleigh looked out the window of the train car, watching the trees and fields roll past them. It had been over three days on the train since they left New York, and Sebastian had said that even after the train ride they'd still need to travel the rest of the way by horse, which would add an extra three days or so. She couldn't understand why Sebastian wanted to go to these "Cheyenne Indians" so badly. She had heard tales from British travelers that the Indians in the Colonies were known to be rather violent, having done many cruel and harsh things to the people who took their land. So, for Sebastian to be so adamant about meeting them just baffled her.

"Ashleigh!" She shook her head and focused on Sebastian. "Hm? What is it?" "I've been talking to you for the past three minutes about where I got my scarf," he said. "Are you alright?" Her face reddened, embarrassed at her air headedness. "Yes, I'm alright. Sorry Sebastian," she said. "My mind has just been elsewhere." She looked back out the window, the trees moving by faster than she could keep track of. "I just don't understand why you're so in need of these people. I mean, all I've ever heard from others is that they're savage people, warriors by nature who cut your scalps off and blame the 'white man' for invading their home." Sebastian's got wide at her remarks, but he quickly eased down. "Yes, I do suppose they have a rather unpleasant reputation. But they are not just warriors. They are also healers and wise folk; they have a culture all their own that is amazing to learn about. And to be fair, settlers from England did leave for a new home and when they found the colonies, they did take their home, and usually by force no less. How would you feel if someone came to your home and started hanging his paintings and drapes along your wall?"

Ashleigh didn't have a response. All of it did make sense, and she suddenly felt ashamed for assuming otherwise. "Sorry. I suppose I may have let other's opinions get the better of me." As she began to slouch back in her seat, Sebastian leaned forward and looked her in the eyes with a smile. "It's alright to be like that sometimes. I assume you've never met any Indians before, have you?" She shook her head in acknowledgement. "And there's nothing wrong with that. It's understandable that you may have doubts about where we're going and so you look to what others have said. But I wouldn't base your thoughts too heavily into what others have said before you. Take what I said for example. Even though I assured you that not all Indians are like the ones you've heard of. But that doesn't mean those Indians specifically don't exist either. There are those who are hateful of those with lighter skin and see them as an enemy, and there are some who do those horrible things you've heard of."

Ashleigh suddenly felt a chill down her spine, feeling more worried than she had before. She placed her hand on her head, rubbing her scalp to make sure it was still attached well. "You're really good at making people feel better have I told you that?" Sebastian laughed and reached for her hand, holding it in between his own. "The point I'm trying to make, is that you should never let other people's opinions and experiences define how you view something. It doesn't hurt to use them as an idea of sorts, but you should always decide for yourself what you think and don't think about something."

He let go of her hands and leaned back in his seat. "Does that make you feel better?" he asked. "I suppose," she said smiling at him. "Still doesn't explain why you're so persistent about going to see them though." Sebastian sighed and turned his gaze to the window. "No, I suppose it doesn't," he said with a smile. Before he could give her a proper answer, he quickly turned to look at young Sybil. "How is she?" he asked. Ashleigh looked over to her side at the child, checking her every which way possible. Since the boat ride she had gotten used to certain patterns and tricks to care for the youngling, even asking other mothers from the ship ride how to properly care for her. She made sure her head was resting properly in the basket she was in, adjusting it every so often when she would squirm more than she should.

"She's doing better since we left New York," Ashleigh said. "I'm still unsure about some things but it's getting easier to handle her. Honestly the hardest part so far was trying to get out of New York without someone questioning why our last names were different from hers." Sebastian got a confused look on his face. "It wasn't that hard," he said confusedly. Ashleigh rolled her eyes and glared at him. "My last name is Briner, her last name is Atkins, and as far as I know you don't even have a last name." She quickly glared at him unsure of him now. "What is your last name?" Sebastian laughed. "Not the point," he said changing the subject. "And besides, it was easiest for me to say that we shared a last name and that we were the child's aunt and uncle, wasn't it?" Ashleigh looked at the young girl, asleep as can be. "I suppose," she said trying to get past the fact that she doesn't know what Sebastian's last name is.

"But anyway, you still haven't told me why we're going to the Cheyenne Indians. Why are you so secretive about this?" Sebastian looked at her and shook his head, as if he were preparing to break some horrible news. "Listen Ashleigh…" before he could answer the train started to slow down, the whistle of the engine blaring in the distance. "Oh, we're here." He got up, reaching for his bag he had put under the seat. "Come on Ashleigh we need to get your luggage before someone takes it by mistake." Ashleigh stood up behind him, angered by his eagerness to hold his answer back. "Sebastian…" "This will sound obvious I know but do remember to grab Sybil on the way out. I would prefer to not forget her on the train." "Sebastian please…" "I can't quite remember where the luggage was stored. Do you remember where it is? I swear my memory is worse than Maxwell's…"

"Sebastian!" He looked back and saw that Ashleigh's face was bright red, her hands clenched into fists. Others on the train looked at them to see why she had yelled, unsure of the sudden commotion. "Ashleigh be careful. We don't want to draw unwanted attention." Before he could finish his sentence, she grabbed his arm and pulled him close to her, bringing his eyes to her own. "I am getting tired of you putting off answering my questions Sebastian. I get that you have your secrets but I'm starting to feel like I can't even trust you with where we're going or why we're even going there." Her expression went from angered to worried in an instant. "Please Sebastian. I want you to trust me." He looked at her guiltily and couldn't shake that he was crushing her in a way. But he could see more people were beginning to stare at them and he was worried about causing a scene. "It's alright everyone," he announced throughout the car. "She hasn't been on a train before, so it startled her." People sighed and went back to their business, some preparing to leave when the train reached a full stop. He pulled Ashleigh close and looked her in the eyes. "I know I'm keeping things a secret from you," he said in a low tone. "But you must understand there are some things I'm just unsure of talking about just yet." He placed his hands on hers, forcing a smile to hopefully feel better. "I give you my word that when we leave this place, I will tell you. Just please, trust me for a little while longer." She pulled her hands away and shrugged, grabbing Sybil's basket. "I suppose that's all I can do for now," she said looking out the window one last time. "Otherwise why did I come on this journey then?"

As the train came to a full stop, Ashleigh began walking towards the exit. "Luggage is in one of the back cars. If I take your bag you can grab mine since its larger." Sebastian silently handed her his satchel began following her. "Alright then," he said following close behind her. "Once we're off the train we'll get a carriage and from there it will only be a few short days, I promise." When they reached the steps of the car Sebastian exited first to help Ashleigh down, reaching his hand out for her to grab. She took it silently, stepping down onto the dirt. "Don't make a girl a promise if you don't think you can keep it Sebastian," she said, giving him a slight glare. Before he could answer, she began walking with a small crowd of people to the luggage car, leaving him there with the car attendant. He couldn't shake the guilt he felt, adding to the other harsh things he's done to those he cares about.

Chapter 3

Without warning, the carriage stopped abruptly, forcing Ashleigh to steady herself and Sybil. "Why'd we stop?" she asked. Sebastian poked his head out of the window, speaking to the driver. "I won't go any further," the man said. His voice sounded odd, deep with an accent she had never heard before. "What do you mean?" Sebastian asked. "It's another 8 miles to the land and we have a child with us. Do you really expect us to walk the rest of the way there?" The driver jumped down and walked to the window. He looked remarkably like Sebastian, only with an unshaven face and scruffy brown hair. His clothes covered in dirt and his boots worn. "Look pal I get you got business out that way with those people, but I don't want none of their trouble. If it helps any, I'll give you one of the horses for your lady and the kid. I got a spare saddle under your seat that she can use, but otherwise your walking from here on." He turned back and looked out towards the remaining stretch of land ahead of them. "You won't be changing my mind. I'm not going out any further." He stepped away from the door, opening it. "Now would you kindly move so I can get the saddle and help the missus?"

Sebastian begrudgingly stepped out and allowed the man to do his work. The man reached his hand out for Ashleigh to grab. "Thank you," she said. "If you don't mind my asking, why won't you go any further?" The man gave her a worried look, and then looked back to the distance. "I know rumors don't get around everywhere, but these people..." Sebastian got the last bag down from the carriage and sighed. "I know these people they're alright. They've helped me before, so I don't see the issue." The man suddenly grabbed Sebastian's arm, a wild look in his eyes. "Just because you think you know them, doesn't mean you don't know who they were. These people have a history in this country, a bloody history at that. Watch yourselves the next time you say that while surrounded by a whole horde of them." Sebastian pulled his arm away, moving towards Ashleigh. "I assure you, I know these Indians in particular, so despite your many worries, I think we're fine." The man walked over and untied one of the horses, reigning it towards the saddle he pulled out. As he placed it on the horse, he continued to give Sebastian a particularly harsh glare. "Keep telling yourself that. But I don't think you should be getting those two involved. Bad things can happen to people like you. And when it does..." he handed the reigns to Sebastian and looked him up and down one more time. "You best make sure you pray to God that it ends quickly.

With that the man climbed back on top of the carriage and rode back the way they came. Sebastian scoffed at the man as he rode off, tying his bag to the horse's saddle. "Honestly, the nerve of that man. I understand being paranoid of the Indians, but to say such things I swear. Don't you agree Ashleigh?" as he turned to look at her, he saw that she wasn't sharing similar feelings. Her face was pale, and her hands were shaking. "Yeah," she said trying to hide the worry in her voice. "Paranoid." Sebastian placed his hands on her shoulders and ushered her to the horse. "Don't worry Ashleigh," he said taking Sybil from her so she could get on the horse. "I give you my word as an Englishman that these people are not that bad. Some yes, but not all." She reached out for Sybil and took her into her lap. She looked as the child remained quiet, unnerved by all the moving around. "Ok," she said as she placed her hands on the basket. She tried to think about something else, anything to clear her head. "Are you going to be ok walking the whole way Sebastian?" she asked. We can take turns if you like. "No, no its quite alright Ashleigh," he said as he placed the last bag on the horses back. You're better at carrying the child and I feel much better walking. Besides it'll give you a chance to relax." He went to the front of the horse and grabbed the reigns, pulling it to go forward. "Don't worry now, just relax. It's only a few miles and then we're there." Take some time and just breathe. Ok?" Ashleigh nodded silently, but deep down she was in some way terrified of going anywhere near these people. But she chose to leave it be and trust him

After about an hour or so they stopped to take a rest at a nearby stream. Sebastian was pouring sweat and the horse began breathing heavily through its nose, sweating almost as much as Sebastian was. As they sat Ashleigh couldn't help but look over her shoulder once or twice, making sure they weren't being watched. "You wouldn't see them coming," Sebastian said. She looked back him, watching him fill his canteen. "They're hunters by trade and they know how to sneak up on their pray, so sneaking up on a pair of travelers won't be much different." Ashleigh's eyes got wide, moving closer to Sebastian. "I'm kidding," he said smiling at her. "Well partially anyway." She glared at him, moving back towards the horse. "Look I know you're worried about everything, but I promise it'll be fine. And besides they're going to give us a warning before they do anything." What do you mean 'warn us?'" she asked.

Suddenly, a group of men rushed out of the nearby brush with spears and bows, yelling in a language foreign to Ashleigh. "What are they saying?" she asked Sebastian. "Well my Algonquian is a little rusty, but I'd say the ruff translation is that they wish to know why we are her, or else they'll do some pretty nasty things to us if we don't tell them." Ashleigh pulled Sybil closer to her and moved back towards Sebastian. "What do you mean by 'nasty things?'" He looked at her and began rubbing his head. "Let's just say that you might want to remain close if you want to keep your scalp attached to your head." They began moving closer, pointing their spears directly at Sebastian. "Well do something soon or else we're not going to last much longer then!" she urged him. Sebastian moved Ashleigh behind him, standing straight and clearing his throat. "We come as friends to the Cheyenne," Sebastian spoke slowly, trying to annunciate his words. They stopped moving and watched him talk, those with bows having their arrows pointed directly at his throat. "We come to meet with a friend in your tribe. His name is Shaman." He picked up a stick and began drawing in the dirt, causing the people to back up in fear. He drew what looked like a large hammer, putting small dots on the side. "Shaman," he said again, placing the stick on the ground.

The men looked between each other, speaking in hushed words. Ashleigh nudged Sebastian, unsure of what was going on, and all he could do was shrug his shoulders. Then, one of the men stepped forward, his hair done in two long braids and a feather sticking up from his hair. He walked up to Sebastian, looking him up and down. His skin was aged, and his eyes worn, as if he'd more than his fair share of conflict and stress. "Who are you?" he asked, his voice heavy and his words stern. "And why do you seek Shaman?" Sebastian smiled and reached into his pocket, pulling out a small charm in the same shape as the hammer he drew. "I am the *Miskwà Inini*, I seek his aid with a personal matter."

The man's eyes got wide, and voices among the others began to murmur, repeating the phrase again and again. The man lifted his hand, signaling the others to lower their weapons. "Forgive us for not recognizing you, *Miskwà Inini*. We have been on the search for intruders of late." Sebastian placed the charm back in his pocket, smiling at the man. "It's quite alright. Is everything alright in the tribe?" The man rubbed the back of his neck, looking around at the nearby brush that he and his companions came out of. "We have had harsh spirits come to the village, rare instances but they've been growing, we thought they might just be tricksters or a Maxemista looking for food, but we think it's something worse." "What kind of worse are you describing?" Before the man spoke, he looked back at Ashleigh, and noticed the young newborn in her arms. "Maybe we should talk about this at a time when the lady isn't here." Ashleigh stepped forward, keeping Sybil close to her. "I hate to interject but I think I have a right to know what monster or evil spirit might be lurking nearby. Also hello my name is Ashleigh and Sebastian seems to have a particularly bad time introducing me to others." Sebastian turned to face her, placing a hand on her shoulder. "Listen Ashleigh," he began. "Most women in the tribes are rather silent, usually staying home and doing home duties. I don't know how they might feel about a woman standing up like this and demanding information. Maybe you should..."

"Sebastian I've saved you from death not once but twice, I helped stop a vampire and two demons, one of which worked under Satan himself, and I've been following you around not knowing much of anything. If there's one thing I should at least know about, it should be what might be trying to kill us in advance before it starts. And if not for me I at least want to know for Sybil. Alright?" Sebastian was silent, unsure of how to answer. "Alright. I suppose you deserve to know just as much as anyone else." He looked back at the man and waved his hand between him and Ashleigh. "I did not catch your name my good sir." The man bowed and held out his hand for Ashleigh. "My name is Avonaco or Leaning bear. It is a pleasure to meet you miss...?" "Ashleigh Briner" she said taking his hand. "Or just, Ashleigh." "Alright Just Ashleigh," he said. "I will tell you both of what we fear is coming after our tribe. But we must return soon before nightfall comes. Let us be on our way and I will tell you as we travel."

He said some phrase to the other men, and they began rushing around one another. Avonaco urged the two to follow him, saying that they had another horse for Sebastian. Sebastian grabbed the reigns of their original horse and as they walked, Sebastian pulled Ashleigh next to him so they could talk. "I'm sorry if I seemed rude to you before. Sometimes these tribes have rules and don't do well with strangers who don't follow those rules." "I understand Sebastian, but I need you to understand that I am myself used to certain rules. I get they some places have certain rules about a woman's place among them, but I'm not just going to stand by like some confused animal. I deserve to know these things just as much as anyone else." Sebastian looked down at the ground, feeling rather guilty. "You mustn't blame him madam," Avonaco said. "He has been many places and has met many people. Most tribes like ours do hold women in a place of service to the home, choosing to keep them there. While most women in our tribe do the same, there are those who stand alongside us as equals, even joining on hunts. He speaks from experience, and all he cares for is to make sure that you yourself are in the best possible situation. Do you understand what I mean Just Ashleigh?" Ashleigh looked at Sebastian, her expression both annoyed and entertained. "Am I always going to be called 'Just Ashleigh' now?" Sebastian laughed. Ashleigh smiled, and looked back to Avonaco. "I do understand," she said.

Avonaco turned back and smiled. "That is good," he said. He turned back to the front and moved a patch of branches out of the way to reveal a set of horses standing next to a large tree. "Now," he said as he motioned for Ashleigh and Sebastian to move ahead of him. "Let us guide you back to our tribe."

Chapter 4

"So, let me make sure I'm understanding this properly," Ashleigh said, keeping her grip on the horse as it was led by Sebastian's own. "You think your tribe has been under the attack of a large monster that was once human but now it isn't?" Avonaco nodded his head in acknowledgement. "And this creature, it feeds on human flesh? But since it was human and therefore still is human like it means it's a…" "A Cannibal yes," Avonaco confirmed. "A poor soul that once ate and hunted like we do, only to now crave the flesh of his fellow man. Once they eat human flesh, they sacrifice their soul and become a Wendigo." Ashleigh gulped and looked down at Sybil, her body tossing and turning in her arms. "I can't imagine anyone becoming that desperate…" she mumbled under her breath. "Do you know who they were?" Sebastian asked. "Before they became this creature?"

Avonaco looked out ahead of them, watching his surroundings. "We believe they may have been a member of a hunting party from some time ago, a woman. She was strong, capable of herself in combat. But after a hunt she did not arrive with her party. Some weeks pass and we find what is left of them, torn apart by teeth alone. All the men were accounted for, but not the woman. We think they were unable to catch any game, forcing them to keep searching; in doing so they may have grown desperate, willing to eat anything to stay alive. And in the end, she was the victor." Ashleigh swallowed her breath, finding it hard to imagine being so desperate for food that one might consider the unthinkable.

"And you're certain it's a Wendigo?" Sebastian asked. Avonaco nodded. "We keep finding tracks surrounding the village, but rarely entering. Food and tools keep disappearing as well, forcing us to spread out our food." Ashleigh looked at Avonaco confused. "I'm confused, how is that a sign of a Wendigo?" she asked. "Couldn't that very well be another Indian scavenging supplies?" Avonaco looked back at her. "We thought that as well, until a few weeks ago, when we found one of our own hunting parties in the woods, torn to shreds." Ashleigh's eyes widened. "Maybe it was a bear?" "Avonaco lifted his hand, stopping all he horses and riders. He walked back and looked Ashleigh in the eyes. "Bears don't cut off a man's head with a dull axe after they rip their throats out." Ashleigh didn't know what to say. Of everything she'd seen or heard she had never heard of anyone doing something like that. "I'm sorry," Ashleigh said. "I didn't know..."

Avonaco sighed, placing his hand on the head of her horse. "It is alright Just Ashleigh," he said giving her a smile. "He died with his spear in his hands, like the warrior he was." He lifted his hand and motioned it forward, urging everyone to move forward. "It hasn't attacked us since, but we are still searching. We will not rest until this creature is slain and put to rest." He moved back to the front of the group, guiding them further. "You know I need to ask you something Avonaco," Sebastian said. "What is it Miskwà Inini?" he asked. "Well I noticed your English is rather fluent compared to most Cheyenne I've met in the past. As far as I knew, Shaman was the only one who could speak fluent English. So, how is it that you speak it so well?" Avonaco laughed, looking back to Sebastian and smiled. "Shaman is not the only Cheyenne to conversate with White Men I assure you. As of recent I've gone with him myself to English markets in nearby towns to learn the ways of your people." "And your chief approves of this?" Sebastian asked in a startled voice. "No, he disapproves, but he also understands that I do it not for personal gain, but for that of the tribe." He turned his attention back to the path, watching the sun float in the sky. "As Shaman were to put it, "Times are changing, and it is best we too do the same"' Sebastian laughed. "How much closer are we?" he asked. Avonaco smiled and pointed forward. "See for yourself."

Ahead of them they could see a hill and as they got closer, they could see the tops of tents rising above them. Within a few minutes they had a full view of the tribe and their home. Ashleigh could see that people were walking back and forth between tents, some carrying meats and weapons, others carrying clothes and charms that looked like they were just made. "These people just live out here all on their own?" she asked Sebastian. "Most of the time yes," he told her. "Sometimes they will trade with other tribes or even go to outer towns further from their home for supplies. But yes, most of the time they stay close to where they make camp." As they walked along the makeshift path created by others, Ashleigh could see they were all staring at them, eyes following them as they went. "Um, are we going to have to deal with what we went through in Ostia and the Basilica again are we?" she asked keeping her hands tight on Sybil. Avonaco looked back at her and smiled. "I assure you they mean well. We do not get many visitors here, especially those with such bright red hair and lighter skin." Sebastian rubbed his hair and shrugged. "I suppose I do look a little strange. But I've been here enough I should be somewhat recognizable. Why would they stare now?" "They may know of you, but I am sure your partner has raised a few eyebrows." Sebastian looked over at Ashleigh, and she looked at her hair and dress. "I don't look that strange do I?" she asked. Avonaco laughed. "Attire like yours with curly black hair? To them it's as strange as wheat colored hair and bright blue eyes."

Ashleigh pulled a stand of her hair and looked around at the women she passed, seeing that their hair was much straighter, left hanging flat or done in long braided tails; as well as their dresses, stopping at knee length and with flat shoes, while she herself wore a dress to her ankles with boots. "I suppose I do seem a bit strange," she muttered, keeping her head low. "Give them time Ashleigh," Sebastian said as he pulled beside her, placing his hand on her own. "They just need some time to get used to you. It took me time to get them to accept me, and you have the same hair color as them at least." Ashleigh smiled, holding his hand as they walked. "I guess you're right," she said, looking up and around at the village. "Hey Sebastian. How will we know when we reach this Shaman's tent?" "Sebastian looked forward, watching for something he'd recognize. "Oh, he doesn't stay in a tent," he said. "Ashleigh looked at him confused, to which he laughed, turning his gaze to his right. "Let's just say a tent doesn't have the space he needs.

Ashleigh followed his gaze, noticing something much larger than any nearby tent. Far behind the tents there stood two structures, one of them a larger tent than the others, taller than even Sebastian while riding his horse; the other, a small log cabin standing about 20 feet from the largest tent. Most of the tents Ashleigh had passed were all plain white with a small entrance in it, but this one was decorated in various drawings, some she recognized and others she didn't; some looked like people and others looked like animals she had never seen before. The log cabin across from it looked more than 30 feet long and possibly 15 feet wide; it stood taller than any horse she'd seen, with a small chimney rising in the back. "Wow," Ashleigh said. "Not what I was expecting." "You took the words from my mouth," Sebastian said admiring the log cabin. "How did you manage to build this without getting moved by any other Americans? And so close to the chiefs Tipi." Sebastian asked Avonaco. They stopped a few feet from the cabin at a nearby post, already set with a few horses. Avonaco climbed down from his horse, tying it down next to another horse. "When we settled here, some White men did come by, trying to ward us off from staying here and urging us to join the others who had gone to the settlements. But Shaman was able to arrange a deal with them, explaining we needed to stay here for the nearby wildlife and herbs. They agreed, as long as we agreed to trade anything useful with any of the nearby settlements."

Sebastian stepped down from his horse, moving to take Sybil from Ashleigh so she could do the same. "Is that the only reason?" he asked. Avonaco smiled, placing his hand on the side of the cabin. "No, it is not," he said." This land is very important to us. Some of the chief's own blood is buried here, as well as sacred hunting grounds. We wanted to return here and rest permanently, but we knew we would have to deal with them. Shaman knew this too, and was able to work something out, and because of that, his cabin rest to the chiefs Tipi." Sebastian looked the building up and down one more time and smiled. "Yes, that does sound like him," he said. "Well, I suppose we should head inside then. Come on Ashleigh, I suppose you should finally meet Shaman." He turned to give her Sybil, only to see that she had been pulled away by a group of women, all of which were mesmerized by her outfit. "Um, Sebastian?" she said trying to pull her head away from one who wanted to study her hair. Sebastian laughed, entertained by just how much of an oddity Ashleigh was to them. "Is this what it was like for you when you arrived the first time?" Ashleigh asked.

"Actually, there were a lot more spears and glares when he first arrived," a deep voice said. Ashleigh turned to see that in the cabin doorway stood a man who looked much different from the other Cheyenne she had seen. His skin was lighter, with long black hair and a shaggy black beard, to which no other Cheyenne had been seen with; he was extremely fit, his body with a likeness to a statue. He wore a large pendant around his neck, a bird carved on in the center. But perhaps the most striking feature about him, were his eyes, and for the simple fact of she could not see them since he wore square black glasses. At his sides hung two large and strange looking hammers, each decorated in beads and with both sides of each covered in a sort of leather.

He walked up to Sebastian, his strides long and pronounced and a slight rattling could be heard from the hammers. "I must say they've taken a faster liking to you than they did him." Sebastian opened his arms offering a hug, to which Shaman returned with a kind hand on the shoulder. "Shaman it's good to see you," Sebastian said with a wide grin. "And it is good to see you as well Sebastian," he said as he pulled Sebastian in for a hug. Ashleigh watched in amazement, shocked at the difference in size between the men. Sebastian stood at six feet tall and one inch, and most of the Cheyenne that surround them stood at a possible five feet and 10 inches, but this man stood over him by another 6 inches. "I see you've chosen to let the beard grow," Sebastian said as he pulled away from Shaman. "Shaman stroked the beard, giving Sebastian sarcastic glare. "And I see you've chosen to keep wearing the same tattered scarf," he said in turn. Sebastian looked at him offended, pulling the scarf close and holding it in his hands. "Why must everyone make fun of the scarf?" he asked looking down at it. "Everyone has something that is theirs and this is what I like to consider mine."

Shaman shrugged his shoulders, looking down at the funny ginger haired man. "I suppose you are right," he said. He turned his gaze to Ashleigh who, like the women surrounding her, all froze when he turned. The group of women disbanded, returning to their original tasks and leaving Ashleigh alone. Suddenly she started to miss the crowd of women hiding her from the large intimidating man. He walked over, stopping within two feet of her and giving her plenty of room to breathe. She looked up at the man who towered over her now. He reached his hand out in gesture for a handshake, politely waiting. "It is a pleasure to meet a companion of Sebastian's," he said in a polite voice. She slowly took his hand and shook it, noticing that despite his beefy stature and large hands, he held hers in a light grasp. "It's a pleasure to meet you," said. Sebastian watched from the side, enjoying seeing his two friends meeting one another, hoping this might help bring some closure to Ashleigh's burning curiosity.

"Well now," Sebastian said motioning back towards Ashleigh. He presented her Sybil, whom she took eagerly. "I'm sad to say that we are not here on the happiest of terms. Shaman, I need to talk to you about the you know what…" Shaman looked at Sebastian and nodded his head. For a moment Ashleigh thought she could see his eyes, but they were quickly covered up by the glasses. "I understand old friend," he said in an almost sad tone. "But I'm afraid I am out of the essential ingredients." He looked to his cabin, watching the smoke rise from chimney. "I was planning on getting some more just before your arrival. Perhaps you would like to retrieve them? You know their appearance better than I do." Sebastian nodded, but the just as quickly shook his head. "I would normally join you, but I don't want to leave Ashleigh by herself..." Ashleigh turned to him, Sybil tossing in her arms. "I'm not a child Sebastian," she said. "I can handle being alone for a little bit. Besides it could give me a chance to see the tribe, meet people."

"Actually," Shaman said interrupting her. "That does give me an idea... One moment." Shaman quickly turned back to the cabin, rushing inside the cabin, leaving the two standing out front. "Excuse me, Miss Just Ashleigh?" She turned to see Avonaco, standing there with a young woman. "I've been meaning to ask. Would you like to take a break from caring for the young one?" Ashleigh looked at him surprised. "You mean Sybil? No, its fine really. I don't mind watching over her." Sebastian stepped over and looked down at the child, watching her sleep. "You haven't had a real break Ashleigh. Maybe you can use this as a sort of recovery moment?" Ashleigh looked down at the little one, her breathing calm and her eyes closed. It amazed her how she could remain so quiet. "I suppose you're right..." she said reluctantly. Avonaco stepped aside to show her the young woman. "This is my Sister, Neha," he said. She bowed her head and smiled. "She is a mother to two, one of which is as old as this one. And I trust her with my life. If there is anyone I trust with a child, it is her." She stepped forward, and moved her arms in the cradle position, waiting for Ashleigh to decide. "Well...Alright." She said as she handed her the baby. She adjusted herself to compensate for the child. "Has she been well breast fed?" the woman asked. Ashleigh blushed, unsure of how to answer; thankfully, Sebastian quickly stepped in. "She isn't the birth mother I'm afraid," he said as he placed his hands on her shoulders. "She was given to us and we've been using alternatives. Bread with water or some diluted milk. Neither of us has the most experience caring for a child..." The woman looked down at the child, lightly turning her cheeks to see how she looked. "She is healthy," she said. "I will feed her as you have. I will make sure she is well when returned to you." She slowly walked off, making sure the child was held properly. Ashleigh watched as she walked away, not taking her eyes off her.

Her stare was interrupted by the cabin door opening, Shaman exiting with two small bags and a piece of paper. "This is a list of the herbs you need, and you can put them in this bag," he said. He handed the two items to Sebastian. "If there is something you cannot find or are unsure of, Avonaco can explain it to you." Avonaco nodded, moving to one of the horses. "But what about…" her sentenced was finished by Sebastian. "What about Ashleigh?" he asked. "Shaman looked down at her and smiled. "While most of the key herbs are unavailable to me, there are some other things I need that are more readily available in the tribe. Ashleigh can accompany me." Her eyes got wide as she looked between Shaman and Sebastian. "I can?" she asked startled. "Yes, you can madam," Shaman answered. He placed his hand on her shoulder, keeping it just short of contact. "You said you wanted to see the tribe, so I suppose I could be your guide of sorts. IS that alright Sebastian?" He looked down at the bag and then at Ashleigh. "I don't have any problems with it," he replied. "But I won't decide for Ashleigh. What do you want to do?" She looked between the two again, unsure of what to do. And then, a thought came to mind, one that might help her. "I have no problems with it," she said looking up to Shaman. "I suppose you lead the way then." Shaman smiled at her, but quickly returned his gaze to Avonaco. "I don't think I need to tell you but be on guard. We don't know where it is right now so be careful. Understand?" Avonaco nodded his head, placing his hand on the spear at the side of the horse. "You have my word," he replied. He climbed up on the horse, offering Sebastian his hand one he steadied himself. After he got settled, Avonaco turned the horse around and began moving onward. "We'll be back soon Ashleigh," he yelled as the moved forward. She waved her hand, assuring him she'd be alright. With that, she followed Shaman into the village, hoping that she would learn about more than just Shaman and his people.

Chapter 5

As they walked, Ashleigh couldn't help but admire the way the Cheyenne lived. Their tipis, while some were plain white, others had a blue or red trim with similar markings to the chiefs own; the people she saw each had beautifully made clothes, with jewelry she had never seen. "I'm guessing this is your first experience with people like this?" Shaman asked. Ashleigh snapped back to reality, blushing at her naïve nature. "I'm sorry, I didn't think I was being that obvious," she said. Shaman laughed, stopping abruptly at a tent with an open entrance. "Its quite alright," he said. He poked his head inside, spoke a few words, and placed his hand inside. When he pulled it out, he held a few small berries which he placed in his bag. "It is understandable that you might be mesmerized by us. It's a nice change from the usual looks of fear and disgust we would normally receive from white folk." Ashleigh looked at him stunned. "What do you mean?" she asked.

He stopped once again and another tent, one which had a woman standing outside with a few pelts and strips of leather. He spoke some more words and she quickly nodded her head and rushed inside the tent. "You aren't from The American colonies, are you?" he asked. She rubbed her arm and looked at the ground. "It's that obvious isn't it?" "With that accent of yours and how you seemingly have no idea why white people would give us dirty looks? No not at all." The woman stepped out again with a few small plants, some with small thorns on them. He took them and said something quick to her, to which she nodded and continued her work. "The history between our people and those who came here after us is long and bloody. This caused others like us to become vengeful and filled with hate, leading to more spilled blood. To have someone from outside this country and appreciate our ways is... refreshing."

They continued to walk, making a few more brief stops before turning around back to the cabin. "Can I ask a question?" she asked. "As long as it does not offend me," Shaman replied. Ashleigh was taken aback for a moment, only for Shaman to laugh it off. "I am merely joking Miss Briner. You can ask me anything." Ashleigh sighed and prepared to ask her question, only to be interrupted by a sudden thought. "How did you know my last name?" she asked. Shaman looked back her with a smile. "Sebastian told me in one of his letters. I believe he sent it just before you left the Basilica." Ashleigh felt a tinge of anger in the back of her mind. "How did he...?" "He sent it out just before you left the Basilica." "Why did..." "He wanted me prepared for your arrival. Of course, as we can see that was sadly not the case." Ashleigh sighed angrily at the thought that Sebastian essentially went behind her back, and so easily at that. "I swear when I see him..." Before she could continue her statement, Shaman stopped and turned around, his body casting a rather large shadow over her. "I understand you are displeased with his actions. But I recommend not getting to upset in public, but perhaps when we reach my cabin you can speak your mind." Ashleigh begrudgingly agreed, continuing to follow Shaman.

"Now what was it you wanted to originally ask me?" She looked up at him, trying to distract her thoughts with the original question. "I was going to ask how you met Sebastian?" Shaman placed his hand to his chin, lightly stroking his beard again. "I do believe we met some time after he began his travels. He was a confused youth, didn't have that scarf yet, and still unsure of the dangers he so eagerly chased after. He spent some time in the tribe and, when he was ready, he left to continue his journey. He would drop by now and again, seeking certain remedies or different pieces of advice, or he would simply want to just come by and say hello to and old fool." Ashleigh was intrigued at what he was saying, until a new questioned plagued her mind. "Wait how old are you?" "Look at that we're here," he said, dodging the question. He walked up to the door and opened it, giving Ashleigh first entry. She entered and was shocked to see what was inside.

Unlike the various tipis and small makeshift blanket covered beds, Shaman's cabin was much more modern. A full bedframe with pillows and a blanket, a furnace with heating plate and a small kettle, and many shelves lined with books and various bottles; some bottles had powder while others had liquid; there were even those that just held more full plants. She noticed that on each window was a interesting looking charm that hung in front of it; it look like a man made spider web, with small feathers and beads hanging from it.

Shaman followed behind her, setting the bag on a small table. "Would you like a glass of tea?" he asked as he pulled out a small kettle and two cups. "N-no I'm fine thank you," she said. She couldn't help but stare at the home, admiring just how much it contrasted to the rest of the village. "Why is-" "My cabin so much different from the rest of the tribe?" he said, finishing her sentence. She nodded, her eyes darting from one thing to another. "Tell me, do you know what an alchemist is?" he asked. "A sort of scientist who makes potions and remedies." "And do you know what a Shamans role in his tribe is?" he asked. She looked at him, watching him pour water into the kettle. "They're the same thing correct?" Only a Shaman is more spiritual while an alchemist is more scientific?" Shaman nodded in acknowledgement. "That's the simple version yes." He reached for one of the shelves and pulled out a flint and steal, striking it inside the furnace. Once lit, he placed the kettle on the hot plate. "I am what you would consider, a mixture of the two," he said. "I do make remedies and potions like an alchemist, but I also am more spiritual with how I continue those remedies and such." He pulled out a small mortar and pistol, placing a few bits of the herbs he received today. "As I grew up, I was taught how to be a proper shaman," he said as he worked. "I was taught by my grandfather, the shaman before me. He taught me everything he knew, making sure I would be the best possible shaman I could be. Only, he never did get to finish his teachings." He finished crushing the herbs and opened the kettle, pouring the contents inside.

"He passed when I was but 14, leaving me in the care of my grandmother. She knew his teaching and continued to teach me in his place, allowing me to experiment as I went and try new things. Over time I learned that there were other shamans like me, only they weren't called shamans. Some doctors and other's alchemists, all serving the same purpose." Which is?" Ashleigh asked. Shaman looked at her as he readied the two glasses. "They sought to help others, be it physically or spiritually. So, when my grandmother followed my grandfather before her, I decided to go on a journey. The village did not agree with it, but

I did not waver." The kettle began whistling, to which he poured the liquid into the cups and walked over to Ashleigh, handing her a cup. She took it, not even caring that she had just before denied any tea. "The reason my house is like this," he continued. "Is because I choose for it to be that way. Both my home and the tribe's home are different, because that is how I choose to have it.

"Does that answer your question?" Ashleigh sipped her tea, not taking her eyes off the man. "More or less," she said. "I was mainly talking about why your home was so much more modern than everywhere else in the tribe but that works too." Shaman laughed loudly, following it up with a sip of his own tea. "That is because I need more space than most shamans do. Hence this cabin of mine." Ashleigh nodded her head, continuing to sip her tea.

"What is this it tastes very good?" she asked. He set his glass down and walked over to the table, pulling out more herbs and placing them down. "A special mixture I made myself. I learned it from a monk in western Asia. His however was made to relax the body and allow for easier sleep, whereas my version is made more for relaxing the nerves and relieving stress." Ashleigh sipped too much at once and began coughing, trying to calm herself. "I'm sorry, did you say stress? I'm not stressed why would you think that?" Shaman turned around, holding a large knife he seemingly pulled from nowhere. "Every breath is heavy, you step with urgency, and your quick temper towards Sebastian going behind your back also gives it away." Ashleigh set down the glass and looked at Shaman, watching as he cut the herbs into smaller pieces. "It's not just... okay yes, it is because of him going behind my back but it isn't just that. He doesn't tell me things. He hasn't explained where he came from or why he does the things he does, and he most certainly hasn't explained why the Basilica seemingly wants nothing to do with him."

Shaman stopped cutting abruptly, causing Ashleigh to halt her voice. "He hasn't told you?" he asked. "No, he hasn't told me. Why do you know too?" Shaman remained silent. "Of course, you know. Everyone knows except for me. Clyde knows, Johnathan knows, and now you know. I wouldn't be surprised if the tribe knows more than I do." "Ashleigh..." he began. "I mean seriously. I trust him but I just wish he would trust me like he trusts other people. I mean I travel everywhere with him you think he would give me the courtesy of at least knowing who he is..." "Ashleigh," Shaman said, much louder and more aggressive this time. She silenced herself, watching Shaman stand there, knife in hand. He looked out the window above the table, seeing the sun set lower in the sky. He placed the knife down on the table, and stood straight, taking a long breath.

"Do you know why I am called Shaman?" he asked. "I'm sorry?" she asked, confused and unsure of where he might be going with the conversation. "My name. Do you know why I am called Shaman and not another name like 'Leaning Bear' or any other name?" She shook her head, unsure of how to answer. Shaman took off his glasses, setting them down on the table. "When I was born," he continued. "I arrived under interesting circumstances. I was born on a harvest moon, one which had also landed on the day of my mother's birth as well." Ashleigh stared at him confused. "And…?" she asked. He clenched his fist, his knuckles turning white. "She died during labor," he said. Ashleigh sat there in shocked silence, unsure of how to properly answer. "It was not easy," he continued. "The chief told me that there were complications during the birth. Complications which would manifest later in my life. He turned to face her, and she could finally see his eyes. They were pure white, with no pupils of any kind. "Others in the tribe thought it was a miracle I survived, others a bad omen since I caused my mother's death, and on a harvest moon no less." He turned back the face the window, returning his glasses to their place. "My father was of the latter party, believing me to be an omen of bad will. The chief urged my father to see it as an opportunity, but he never got passed it." He went back to cutting up herbs, speaking while he did so. "He then took his own life, believing that he was destined to join my mother early on. I was only a few years old at the time…" He shook his head, refocusing his train of thought. "I was later entrusted to my father's parents, who saw it as an opportunity to raise me in memory of my mother and father. At the time, they had seen I was a much larger child than most, and thusly they decided to name me after my father in his memory, *Otoahnacto* or Bull Bear. But I have since referred to myself as Shaman, for who I am is someone he did not see as a son. They believed I may have been a gift sent down by our creator at the cost of my mother and father. That's a fun way of saying I am responsible for both my parents' deaths isn't it?"

He wiped his hand across his face, a bit of liquid visible along the back of his hand. Ashleigh stared at him in shock, completely unsure of what just transpired. "Why are you telling me all of this?" she asked. He set the knife down and looked back at her, his knuckles white and his cheeks red. "To show you the trust you lack with Sebastian," he said. "And to show you that sometimes its hard for people to speak the most painful of truths." He turned to the herbs and scooped them in his hand. "It's taken me years to come to terms with all of that. Having experienced all that pain at such a young age. Of course, calling myself Shaman instead of Thunder Child helped." He placed the herbs into a small bowl and shook his head once more. "The point is, it takes time for someone to be ready to say all of that. You must give him time to come to terms with what he worries about telling you. Give it time." Ashleigh refocused her thoughts and knew what to say. "I understand," she said. "But it's been months since we met, almost a year. If he isn't ready now, then when will he be?"

Shaman took the pistol and mortar and continued to crush the herbs together in the bowl. "As I said you must give him time…" But how much time is enough?" she asked. I'm worried that one day I'm going to travel with him and end up a gawking bystander like that woman in the dress…" Shaman stopped what he was doing, the pistol clinking with the bowl. "What woman?" he asked. "It was a woman at the Basilica. She was there while we waited for Maxwell and John, she had two small children with her. Sebastian kept staring at them strangely…" Shaman set the bowl down and placed his hands on her shoulders, a panicked expression. "Are you sure that's who you saw?" he asked urgently. "Yes why?" she asked. He let her go and went over to a table, taking his glass of tea with him. He took a long sip, set it down, and look Ashleigh in the eyes.

"If I tell you, do you promise to talk to him about it after you leave the tribe?" She looked at him confused, unsure of what he was talking about. "His past if I tell you about his past do you promise to talk to him about what I tell you after you finish what you need to do here?" Ashleigh looked at him surprised. "Are you sure he'll be alright with that?" she asked. "I mean it is his past…" "Sebastian knows that I wouldn't tell you if I didn't think it was important and right now, I believe you have a right to know. Now do you wish to know about who Sebastian is as a person or not?" Ashleigh looked back and forth between Shaman and the door, unsure whether to respect his wishes or have Shaman tell her everything. Instead she took the middle route. "Tell me what you think I need to know," she said. "You decide how much I hear and how much you keep to yourself. Okay?" Shaman smiled at her, understanding now why Sebastian chose to bring her along. "Alright then," he said. "Let us begin."

Chapter 6

Shaman offered the bed to Ashleigh. She took it, and Shaman himself took upon sitting on a nearby stool. He set his glasses down on a nearby nightstand, his eyes visible for Ashleigh to see. He took a deep breath and looked her in the eyes, his own like empty clouds watching her. "The things I am going to tell you should not be taken lightly, and because of that I ask of you two things." Ashleigh nodded her head in acknowledgement. "Do not think of Sebastian any differently than how you do now. And when I am finished telling you these things, I simply ask that you talk to Sebastian afterwards. Not right after, but before you leave. Do you understand? I want you to be sure before I begin."

Ashleigh sat for a moment, looking at the floor beneath her. After all these dying questions and a need to know Sebastian's past, it seemed that now she felt afraid of the truth. All this secrecy and worry, maybe there was a reason she had to wait. But despite the concern, something inside her told her she needed to know. "I'm ready," she said. "Tell me the truth about who Sebastian is."

"Sebastian didn't have an easy life," he began. "He was born on the streets of London, a beggar's boy as he put it. Didn't know a lot about his father, only that he was a dock worker while he was growing up. But when it came time for his mother to give birth to a

119

pair of twins, a terrible illness struck his place work, killing many workers and leaving many families broken. His family was one of them, and with no man to head the house they were left to the streets. He told me that over time he started caring less of others, only wanting to keep what was left of his family safe.

"One day when he was just 14, two men came across his alley that he stayed on; one of them was an older gentleman with grey hair and a beard. He towered over the child and asked him, 'Why do you live like this my boy?' The boy responded to him, 'My father can't help my family anymore, so I do it in his place.' 'Don't you want to live your own life?', the old man asked him. The boy looked up at him and said, 'My life isn't as important if there is someone else's life who needs helping.' The man then leaned down and looked the boy in the eyes. He could see that this boy had grown up very hard, being given more responsibility than anyone would have needed at his age. 'What if I told you I could give you a life of your own, while still helping your own family in the process?' The boy looked between the man and his family. 'Why should I trust you?' the boy asked. The man then pulled out a small wooden cross out of his pocket, handing it to the young boy. 'A man of god has no right to lie to a child in need,' he said with a smile.

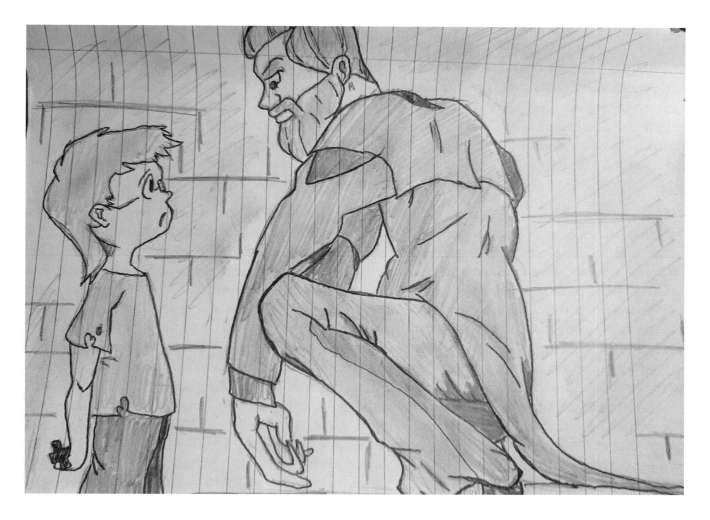

"The boy looked between the man and his mother, watching her struggle to care for all three of her children. 'What would you have me do?' he asked the old man. The man stood up straight, taking a long look at the woman and her two young children; the boy's siblings were no younger than the boy himself. "Come with me to my church. There you can be taught skills that will improve your life from here onward.' He leaned down and placed his hand on his shoulder, turning him to face him family. 'And while you are there, we will ensure that your family is cared for properly. I promise.' The boy looked between the old man and his family, thinking of how he only wanted the best for them. 'Okay,' the boy said looking at the old man. 'I'll go with you. But only if you make sure my family is safe. Okay?' The old man moved the child away and towards the street. 'I give you my word that we will do our best to watch over them.' He looked to the other gentleman, a tall man with long black hair. 'See that they are well cared for Francesco.' The man nodded and walked toward them, offering the boy's mother his hand. As they walked, the boy fiddled with the small cross, noticing the finely carved nature of it. 'Tell me boy, what is your name?' the old man asked. The boy looked up and at the time, thought he saw the face of a man that he thought that he could trust. 'Sebastian,' he said. 'What do I call you?' he asked in turn. 'My name is Maxwell,' the man said. 'And I hope you and I can become friends.'

"When he first arrived, Sebastian noticed that the church did not behave like the ones he knew in England. They wore black dusters rather than the traditional dress attire or white robes; the men and women there wore long black coats covering tailored clothes. 'Why do you not wear the clothes of a priest?' Sebastian asked. Maxwell looked down and smiled. 'We are much more than priests my boy,' he responded. 'We do bless people and perform sermons yes, but we do more than just spread the word of god.' He led Sebastian to an open courtyard, where he could see people training with various weapons, swords and crossbows; he saw men carving stakes and boiling large cauldrons of Water, dipping crosses and filling bottles with it. 'There are creatures in this world that follow the devil's path, and because of this we act as the force that stops them. We do what others cannot, purging the evil out of this world. That my boy, is what we will teach you. 'But why me?' Sebastian asked. 'I am but a boy from the streets. Why would you want to bring me to a place like this?' Maxwell stopped and bent down to look Sebastian in the eyes. 'My boy I see something special in you. Something that many people here lack. You may be a boy from the streets, but I think you can become something great.' He stood up, continuing to walk. 'And besides. I simply could not leave a young man to sit on the streets.' He stopped at a table being run by a man older than Maxwell, a sewing needle in one hand and a piece of thread in the other. 'Do you have it ready?' he asked. The old man nodded and pulled out a small duster, sized to fit a child just larger than Sebastian. He took it, offering it to Sebastian. 'Try it on,' Maxwell said. Sebastian put his arm through the first sleeve, noticing that it was soft and comfortable on the inside. He put the coat on the rest of the way, the sleeves just too long for his arms. 'How does it fit?' Maxwell asked. Sebastian spun in a circle, the back of the coat dragging behind him. 'It's big,' he said with a smile. 'You'll grow into it,' Maxwell said. 'And when that one gets too small, we'll fit you for a new one. One that fits you just right.' He walked forward and placed his hand on Sebastian's head. 'Tell me. Do you want to learn here? To learn how to stop the things that could hurt your family?' Sebastian looked down at the coat, and then back at Maxwell. For the first time in a long time, he felt like he had someone to look up to again. 'Yes. I do want to learn so that I can keep my family safe.' Maxwell smiled at the boy. 'Then let us begin.'

"After some time, Sebastian became highly regarded in the church, becoming well known among others as Maxwell's prized pupil. He mastered all the studies the church had to offer, excelling much faster than most others before him. During his time there, he would try to learn of his family, wishing to meet them and see how they are, but Maxwell would always tell him that they were alright, wishing for him to focus on his studies. After two years Maxwell finally told him they had left some time ago, his mother stating that he had a better place at the church than with them. He was shocked, wanting certain proof of his mothers leaving. Maxwell provided a letter from his mother, explaining everything. He knew her handwriting, even after so long of not seeing her. So, he accepted it, moving on with his studies.

"One day, on his 19th birthday, Maxwell came up to Sebastian and told him that there was something important for him to do. When asked what it was, Maxwell only told him that it was his final test. He then took Sebastian to a tall tower in the church, one that had a winding staircase leading down underground. As they walked, Maxwell talked, speaking about the years Sebastian had spent at the church leading up to this moment. 'Every member of the church must show their loyalty, and to do so they much complete a test to show that they are true to the cause of the church. That is what you are doing today.' Sebastian followed him, unsure of what he was saying. 'But I have followed your ways since I was but a child. What test could I possibly take to prove my loyalty?' Before he could Maxwell could answer, they reached a large doorway, and on that door was a picture of two wings; one, white and full of life, the other black and tattered. 'I know you have done everything I asked of you, and all of it in the name of the church. Now, I ask of you one more task, and then you will have fully proven yourself. Will you do this?' Sebastian looked at the door, feeling a rather uneasy presence from it. But he still felt he could trust Maxwell. A grave mistake that would be.

"Sebastian accepted, agreeing to Maxwells final task. Maxwell opened the door to reveal a large room; it was a study, bookshelves lining the walls. At the center of the room stood a group of men and youths, all watching them as they entered. Sebastian could feel their eyes, watching him with anticipation. As they neared, the men parted ways to reveal a startling sight. There on their knees, were a woman and her two children; they looked starved and fearful, watching them come closer. 'Do you recognize them Sebastian?' He looked at them, unsure of who the children were. But he knew the woman, her image burned into his memory; it was his mother, or rather a shell of her, frail and shaking like an abandoned dog. He took a closer look at the children next to her, and could see the familiar shape of their faces, the eyes that once looked to him for protection.

"'What...the hell is this Maxwell?' Sebastian closed his hands into fists, turning slowly to face his mentor. 'I told you to care for them, not starve them and put them in this condition.' 'I did as you asked,' he said, his tone still and uncaring. 'I cared for them-' Sebastian rushed towards him, grabbing him by the collar of his coat and pressing him against one of the bookshelves. The men and children around them watched in bewilderment, some reaching for their swords. 'How in Gods name is this caring for them?' he yelled as he pressed him into the shelf. 'You said you would care for them and then they left to leave me here. You told me-' 'I told you what you needed to hear Sebastian,' he said. He was unphased by the outburst, acting as calm as he ever did. 'This was all done in the pursuit to make you who you are today. I lied to you yes, but only so you could focus on your studies. You needn't the distraction of someone else's wellbeing...' 'That's my mother you son of a...' He caught himself, choosing not to curse in the lord's house. 'How is this supposed to be a test? Are you testing my patience because I can assure you, I'm on the brink of snapping your neck.' Men inched closer, their hands resting on the hilts of their blades. Maxwell lifted his hand, ordering them to stand down. They backed away, and he gestured for Sebastian to let go of him so that he could explain.

"'This test is one that should help you overcome your past and move forward and think of only your duties to the church. You spent a large part of your youth on the streets, caring for others and not putting your own desires first. With that in mind, consider what you've done since then. You have stepped up and become something more than just a caretaker to your mother and siblings. You've become something great and the goal of this test is to help you see that.' He went to place his hand on Sebastian's shoulder. 'You've been like a son to me Sebastian, and I simply wish the best for you...' Before his hand could touch him, Sebastian snatched it mid-air. 'Caring for me doesn't mean keeping my own mother and siblings hidden away and treated like this.' He stepped back, walking towards her mother. 'Mother its me, Sebastian, I'm going to take you away from here.' He reached his hand towards her, but as she looked up at him, her eyes widened and she smacked him away, rushing away from him. Confused, he reached for his brother and sister, but they too backed away, treating him as if he were the plague.

"'Why do they fear me Maxwell?' Maxwell walked towards a nearby shelf, reaching for a drawer. 'Over time they tried to resist and seek escape. We didn't want them to fight back so we taught them to learn their place.' Sebastian looked closer and could see bruises on her mother, old ones, but there nonetheless. 'Over time they learned that our uniform is to be feared. So as far as I can see it, they learned a valuable lesson I think.' Sebastian stood up slowly, forcing his body from charging Maxwell again. He turned around to see Maxwell was standing there, a gun in his hands. He grabbed the barrel and motioned it towards Sebastian, wanting him to take it. He took it, keeping his finger away from the trigger. 'Do you think giving me this is wise? Considering how I feel right now I am very much tempted to shoot you.' Maxwell laughed, walking towards his mother. 'Oh no, it isn't me you are going to shoot.' He grabbed his mother by her hair and pulled her forward, another man grabbing his siblings by the collar of their shirts. Sebastian pointed the gun to Maxwell, who simply lifted his mother in front of the barrel of the gun. 'You're going to shoot them Sebastian.'

Sebastian didn't know how to respond, his emotions scattered between anger, concern, and utter disbelief. 'What makes you think-' 'You will shoot them Sebastian,' Maxwell stated, cutting him off. 'This church is your life now. And these three don't see you as anyone except one of us.' He pushed the woman closer to the gun, her forehead pressing against the end of the barrel. 'You have nowhere else to go and your life is here, and you belong here. And I think you'll do what you should do.' Sebastian lowered the gun, looking between it and his mother. There were so many emotions rolling around inside him, but deep down he knew what he dad to do. 'You're right Maxwell. I will.' He took the gun, aimed it at the ceiling, and fired. Everyone in the room looked at him shocked, hushed whispers among them. 'The commandments state that and I quote, 'Thou shalt not kill' and

'Honor thy mother and father.' And you are not my father. So, release my mother.' Sebastian dropped the gun to the ground, Maxwell's eyes looking between it and Sebastian. 'If you do this, you are hereby ordered to leave, and you will no longer be seen as a member of this church.' Sebastian stepped forward locking eyes with his teacher. 'I don't see a problem with that then.'

"Maxwell shook his head, tightening his grip on the mother's hair. 'I really hoped you'd be wise Sebastian.' He pulled out a gun from his coat and aimed it to the woman's head. Before he could react, Maxwell pulled the trigger, ending her in an instant. A man stepped from the crowd and followed suit, drawing a pistol and shooting his sister, leaving the man holding his brother to use his free hand and do the same. Sebastian stood there, his mothers blood splashed onto his face and soaking his clothes. Maxwell let her body fall the floor, placing the gun back in his pocket and pulling out a handkerchief. 'Escort Sebastian out of the Basilica and give him a fresh coat and supplies. You're welcome to return Sebastian. I hope you learn your lesson in time. Suddenly, two men grabbed Sebastian by the arms and began pulling towards the stairs. He resisted, trying to fight back and rush Maxwell, but it was to no avail. As he was dragged, a young boy with blonde hair watched as he was taken from the room, unaware of the conflict that truly happened in front of him. Sebastian kicked and scream, cursing Maxwell in every way imaginable. But the damage was done, and Sebastian would never be able to forget what had happened."

Ashleigh stood in silence, her eyes wide and her jaw hanging open. "Oh my god..." she said, unable to fully comprehend what she had just heard. "That's why he is so touchy about saying it. And to think those people... Why would any of them follow Maxwell so blindly? And did they all do that to their oved ones? Oh God John..." "John didn't kill anyone I can assure you of that," Shaman clarified. "Everyone's test is different, depending on how they arrived there. As Sebastian put it, they all had to sacrifice something to prove their loyalty. And as to why they follow him, Maxwell uses the word of God. People want something to believe in and they will do anything to prove their worth if it means they're in the good graces of their god." Ashleigh began pacing back and forth, thoughts racing across her mind. 'That's why he was so adamant about going back this whole time, and that woman with the kids must have reminded him of his family." "Yes," Shaman said, his voice sounding distant. "Also, why did you panic the way you did when I mentioned the woman?" Shaman's gaze turned away. "It just made me think of what happened to Sebastian and how they looked at you, when most anyone there just looks at him. That's all I suppose..."

Ashleigh stared at him for a moment, but soon dismissed the thought and returned to the pressing thoughts she had on her mind. "Why would he ever return there? They killed his mother and siblings. Shouldn't that mean he would have abandoned any and all things to do with them?" Shaman took another sip of his tea, rubbing his finishing the cup. "He holds a grudge against Maxwell, but not the church. The church wasn't responsible for killing them, only Maxwell and his colleagues; he said that the only reason he ever goes there now is information or help. The last time he went there was four years ago I believe, before he met you; he needed to speak to John about how to take care of a certain demon, but otherwise he doesn't go there often." "Ashleigh was still trying to process the information, having more questions than Shaman had answers. "You have many questions I know," he said. "But I don't have the right nor all the information to say what you want to hear." Ashleigh walked back to the bed, resting her head in her hands. "This is a lot to take in I know, but you can't simply rush learning all the answers. Give it time, and you will get the answers you need."

Ashleigh sat there in silence, her mind like a raging storm. All of Sebastian's behaviors suddenly made sense, all the things he does and all the unexplained conflict he had with everyone besides John. Suddenly everything pieced together, and inn her mind she felt as if she had broken a piece of Sebastian's trust. She didn't know what to think. "I...I don't know what to think right now. What do I do until I talk to him?" she asked. "Act as you normally do with him. The best thing you can do is wait and find a proper time to talk to him. Do you understand?" Ashleigh looked at the ground for a moment, and then back at Shaman. "Alright... I suppose I will." He smiled at her and stood up, walking over to the door. "That's good," he said. "Because he's going to be here in a few moments."

Ashleigh's eyes widened, panic suddenly overtaking her. She rushed over to the window and saw Sebastian walking towards the cabin, carrying a basket of herbs and with Avonaco close behind him. "I don't think I can do this," she said. "Maybe you should tell him you admitted to me what happened. Or better yet, you should tell him to tell me, that way he is honest about it and all will be fine and..." Shaman grabbed a small jar filled with yellow liquid that splashed against the glass as he carried it. He took the lid off and lifted it under her nose. Ashleigh stopped mid-sentence, retching away from the jar. "What is that God awful smell?" she asked, her eyes filling with tears. "It smells like a bag of rotten onions mixed with a dead rat." Shaman put the lid back on the jar, placing it on the shelf he retrieved it from. "That my dear, is jarred Skunk Spray. It has its uses, and, don't ask how I have it." He stepped up to Ashleigh, towering over her. "Do not overthink what you will do. I can't nor will tell Sebastian what you know. I simply set the martyr for you two to finally be honest with one another." She wiped her eyes, looking up at him. "You'll know when to talk to him. Understood?" She nodded her head, to which Shaman raised an eyebrow in uncertainty. "I give you my word Shaman. I'll wait." He smiled, walking to open the door. "Good, because I do not want to open that jar again."

He opened it to reveal Sebastian holding his hand up, prepared to knock. "You never let me knock," he said smiling. "Why?" "It's just one of my joys I suppose," Shaman responded. "You retrieved everything I needed then?" he asked. Sebastian entered the cabin, placing the basket on his table. "Yes, and I made sure to get enough so that if you make a bad batch you won't need us to grab more." Shaman laughed, moving to adjust his glasses. "I don't make bad batches and you know that. "Sebastian smiled, but only for a moment. He sniffed the air, turning to directly face the jar of yellow liquid. "Did you open it?" Shaman didn't answer, only looking to Avonaco. "Oh, Shaman why'd you open the jar? Honestly every time you open the damned thing it smells like sour piss in here." He turned back to see Ashleigh, who just stared at him. "I'm sorry he opened that, sometimes he does it to play a prank when I arrive and…" As he spoke, Ashleigh toned out most of what he said, her mind focused on how she would talk to him. Different phrases came to mind, but all were replaced by a potential response from Sebastian, all of which made her worry even more. She lost track of thought until Sebastian finally shook her shoulder. "Are you alright?" he asked. "You looked almost like a corpse. Is there something you want to talk about?" She shook her head, looking to Shaman, who lowered his head to see over his glasses, the white staring right at her. "Yes, I'm… fine," she said. "The smell was rather off putting and I just didn't know how to handle it." She looked up at him and smiled. "As you were saying?" Sebastian looked between Shaman and Ashleigh, contemplating his next words. "I said that Shaman once opened the jar and held it under my nose while I slept. It was an unpleasant awakening I can assure you of that."

That night the village was having a celebratory gathering in light of Sebastian's arrival, though Shaman explained that it was also meant to cleanse any tension among others in the tribe. Ashleigh understood what he meant, remembering how the Chief wanted nothing but peace when the Strigoi was running amok. He said it would involve a passing of a pipe and celebratory dancing. While Ashleigh was intrigued about everything the Cheyenne did, her mind was distracted by other pressing matters. She watched as Sebastian helped another tribe member gather firewood for the pyre they would set up, since it was getting later in the day.

"How are you handling it?" a voice said. She turned to see Avonaco standing next to her. She refocused herself to watching Sebastian work. "Better," she replied. "Still getting used to everything in the village. You all have such a unique lifestyle I've never seen anything like it." He laughed, looking over the village. "Most of your people don't care to learn or even know anything about our people. But when *Miskwà Inini* arrived, it introduced us to something new." Ashleigh looked at him surprised. "And what is that?" she asked. "Hope," he said. "Shaman believes this country will face a great tragedy and our people will be in the 'cross-fire' as he put it. Believing that something will happen here that will place us in the middle of a great tragedy."

Ashleigh turned to him, stunned by what he said. "Why are you telling me that?" she asked. He turned to her and smiled. "I hoped it would help distract your mind from its current struggle." Ashleigh sighed, and turned her eyes to Shaman. "He told you then?" she asked. "Only some of it," he replied. "I asked him not to tell me everything you are going through." He began to walk away, but Ashleigh stopped him before he could. "That's surprisingly polite of you. Why?" He turned back and smiled. "It is not my quest, and so I do not seek the answers the questions that you are asking." She was surprised at his nature, but was thankful for the way he treated her.

"I am going to see my sister. Would you like to come with me? You can check on your offspring." Ashleigh blushed, caught off guard by the sudden comment. "She's not my offspring… I mean she is in a way, but she isn't… Yes, I would like to come with you." She began following him, watching everyone around her work hard to get everything done. As they walked, Avonaco would glance at her every so often, smirking once and awhile. "Does something amuse you?" she finally asked. "I'm simply surprised you haven't asked anything about Shaman yet. I am aware he explained his origins, but I'm sure you must have at least some questions." She took a moment to consider, not quite sure if there was anything she wanted to ask, until she remembered Shamans parents. "He said both of his parents are… gone. Did they really die the way he says they did?" Avonaco's smirk faded, his gaze turned to face her. "I was not there to witness it, but my father before me was there.

"Our fathers were close, having hunted and fought side by side. They were like brothers born from the same tree. But when Otoahnacto met his partner, he saw someone he could not be without. When they planned to have a child, they prayed for a son, one who would make our tribe proud. But as the birth drew near, my father told me that the mothers health was weak; she was strong willed, but her body did not follow that path. So, when Shaman was born, it took her life to give him his own.

"Otoahnacto did not take it very well, believing him to be a sign of bad will, his birth being on a harvest moon. My father tried to tell him that it was a sign for him to raise the child in her name. But when he saw the child was blind, he was certain the babe was a bad omen. He did try to raise the child, with the help of the boy's grandmother and grandfather, but he never seemed to truly want to care for him; it was as if he resented the boy.

"He later took the cowards way out, though no one blamed him. His soul was filled with grief and nothing would sway his thoughts. Shaman was only a child, not fully aware of the situation, not learning the extent until his grandfather passed." Ashleigh looked at him in disbelief, unable to comprehend the idea of such a turmoil. "Shaman doesn't express that story often, only with those he's known long enough to trust. His telling to you when you'd only just met, shows he puts much faith in you. And I see why." "You put such praise on my shoulders it makes me sound important," she said, turning her gaze to the ground. "Well you are important. You mean much to Miskwà Inini, which therefore extends to us as well. He stopped and placed his hand on her shoulder, looking her in the eyes. "You are much more than you give yourself credit for."

Their moment of bonding was cut short by a scream, one which caused Avonaco to react with urgency. "Neha," he said. He quickly ran in the direction they'd been walking. Ashleigh lifted her dress and followed him as fast as possible. When she caught up to him, she could see the carnage. Avonaco stood in front of a tipi that was torn to shreds, pieces of fabric on the ground and red splatters in the dirt. Two other Indians were carrying a blanket and covering someone, to which Ashleigh caught a glimpse and had flashbacks to Ireland. Avonaco rushed to the body, speaking to fast for Ashleigh to understand. One of them shook their head and pointed to a group of women huddled together. He rushed over to see that in the center of their group was Neha, his sister; she had a cut on her forehead and scratches covering her body.

"Are you alright?" he asked, kneeling to check on her. "I am alright brother, just barely. But…" She looked to Ashleigh, her eyes widening. "I'm sorry ma'am. I tried to keep her away, but she…" Ashleigh walked to the tent and saw an empty basket with a familiar looking blanket inside. Ashleigh felt something she hadn't felt before, a feeling of urgency, rage, and fear all together. "Who took her and where is she?" she asked, her voice shaky. Neha looked at the ground, afraid to answer. "Neha who took her?" she asked again. "The Wendigo," a voice said. Ashleigh turned to see a man standing behind her who, when seen, caused everyone around them to stop and make way. He wore a heathered head piece that hung behind him and past his knees, with two small horns on each side; he wore leather clothes and had beads hanging from the sides. Avonaco stood, not leaving his sisters side as the man walked closer to them. "Are you injured?" the man asked. Neha looked up, her tears mixing with the blood dripping down her forehead. "Yes," she said. The man nodded his head, turning to Avonaco. "Gather any silver weapons, knives and spears especially. Gather all the men and prepare them for a hunt."

The man turned to face Ashleigh. "We will end this beast tonight, and retrieve your infant," he said looking at her. "Not without me you aren't," she said, feeling the emotions in her body rise. "Ashleigh wait a moment." She turned around to see Sebastian and Shaman standing behind her. "This is the chief I don't think you should argue…" "Look your… chiefness," she said, choosing to ignore Sebastian's warnings. "I don't know what you have your women do in times like this, but I'm not going to sit here and wait for you to return. Why did it even take Sybil to begin with?" Avonaco stepped forward to answer, only to be cut off by the chief. "It smelt new blood, and your child was easy prey. We will get her." He went to walk away, but Ashleigh cut him off. She heard Sebastian hold his breath, along with everyone else watching her. "With all due respect sir, I will not sit and wait. What I understand is that this Wendigo is deadly, and you're going to need help to kill it. If there are steps to kill it then fine, I'll follow them. Give me a knife and I'll kill it myself if I must. But I will not just sit and wait like a simple house maid." It was utter silence, everyone's eyes on Ashleigh and the chief. The chief eyed her, glancing between her and Shaman. He lifted his coat, pulling out a knife. Sebastian stepped forward but was stopped by Shaman. Ashleigh didn't move an inch, holding her place. The knife was silver, with a leather wrapped handle and two beads hanging from the bottom. The chief looked at it for a moment, and then dropped it into the ground; it landed just inches from Ashleigh's feet. "Actions speak louder than words," he said.

He walked off, everyone around them rushing around to prepare. Ashleigh picked up the knife, noticing that it was a well-made blade. "Are you crazy?" Sebastian asked. "You cannot just talk to a chief like he's some drunk patron at the bar...." Before he could finish his sentence, Ashleigh grabbed him by his jacket collar. "Sebastian listen now and listen good. I am not in a mood to just sit around and wait while all of you go hunting for Sybil, a child we've both been caring for. We may have only had her for a short while, but I am very much not prepared to lose her, Understood?" Sebastian was awestruck, having not seen her get this upset with him. "I understand," he said, lifting his hands in surrender. She let him go, placing the knife in her belt loop. "Good," she replied.

Chapter 7

That night Ashleigh saw the village prepare for what almost seemed like war. She watched as they gathered weapons and horses, covering their faces with paint in black and red shapes. Neha continued to apologize for failing Ashleigh, saying that she should have done more to stop the Wendigo, but Ashleigh reassured her that she did the best she could. She herself understood how hard it can be to defend oneself from a blood thirsty monster. All during this, Sebastian continuously pestered her as to whether she should actually go, fearing that she may have too much emotional stake in this. "I care about Sybil just as much as you," he said. "But I don't want you rushing into this on grit and emotion alone." "I understand your concern Sebastian, but I will not change my mind. We promised to watch over her until we found a safe home for her and now she's in the hands of a flesh craving cannibal." She stopped to see the chief speaking to Avonaco, placing his hand on his shoulder. "And if I did choose to stay it would rather ruin that big scene I made in front of the chief."

Sebastian looked at the chief, looking more nervous than before. "I still can't believe you did that. Had anyone else done that, they would have most assuredly been killed." "Why wasn't I killed then?" she asked, pulling out her knife to examine it. "And why did he give me this?" She brushed her finger along the blade, feeling the grain of the blade; whoever forged this must have been well taught in their craft. "I don't know," Sebastian said. He offered his hand to see the blade, to which she handed it over. "This doesn't look like a traditional Cheyenne blade, though it does have the traditional beads and hand wrap."

His sentence was cut short by Shaman walking towards them. She began to wonder just how he was able to see, despite being blind. "Are you both ready?" he asked. The two nodded, Sebastian returning the knife to Ashleigh. "So where is the creature?" Ashleigh asked. "Some nights ago, one of the hunters discovered a path leading to a cave we had been unaware of. As they got closer, they heard a rising growl coming from the cave. They left just as quick as they had found it, though at the time they believed it to be a bear den. But now it seems to be the best possible resting place for the beast." "Yes, and we should prepare to arrive there by dusk," Avonaco stated, coming from behind them with a rifle slung over his shoulder. "It will still be asleep by then, so we should try our best to kill it before the night is at its apex." He grabbed the reigns of a horse and mounted it, turning it to face the others. "If you want to save that child in time, we need to leave as soon as possible." As if on cue, the others set to travel with them began to pass by them. "Are you sure you wish to stay Shaman?" Avonaco asked. "Your skill could be most helpful when we arrive." "This beast will be dangerous, but I do not believe I am needed." He turned and smiled to Ashleigh. "Even if I am not there you will not be truly alone." Ashleigh looked at him confused. "What do you mean?" He simply smiled and walked away, leaving them to prepare. "Best of luck young Ashleigh. Try not to die." She turned back to see Sebastian with a horse. He jumped on and offered her his hand. "Shaman was joking right?" she asked, sitting behind him. Sebastian laughed. "Well... he isn't wrong. We should get going." Ashleigh sighed and wrapped her arms around Sebastian's waist. "If we die today, I'm going to kill you," she said as he snapped the reigns on the horse.

"How much further?" Sebastian asked, keeping his hands tight on the reigns. "Just a few more yards, and then we should be able to see the cave." Avonaco replied. Ashleigh watched him pull the gun from his shoulder, resting it on the neck of the horse. She could see all the men around her preparing themselves. "Are you sure we can handle this?" she asked Sebastian. He turned to face her, giving her a forced smile. "To tell the truth, I've never encountered a Wendigo. Shaman spoke of them in the past and I heard tales of them from other tribes. But frankly, they are a mystery to me. But we're with people who know how to kill the creature. So, I think we are at our best... I hope." Ashleigh sighed and looked at the passing trees. "What did Shaman mean when he said we wouldn't truly be alone?"

Sebastian took a moment to think before answering. "He believes that everyone is protected by some spiritual force. He says different lands have different ways of looking at it, but he sees it as a spirit from long ago is watching over us, until our proper end is near."

She took a moment to think it over, though her, though her thought was cut short when Avonaco suddenly raised his hand, stopping all the riders. She looked ahead of them and saw the cave. She could also see a small trail of blood going into the café itself. Avonaco got off the horse and tied it to a nearby tree, others following by example. After the horses were tied down, everyone readied their weapons. Some had spears tipped in silver, others like Avonaco carried rifles, filling them with black powder and silver bullets. She looked down at her blade, noting how it seems to be the only pure silver weapon among them. Before she could consider its significance further, Avonaco stepped forward, motioning others to gather with him. "We must kill it as quickly as possible. We only have until the sun rests and it will be at its strongest. Do we understand?" everyone nodded. Avonaco turned to Sebastian, seeing he did not carry a weapon. "How do you plan to defend yourself, *Miskwà Inini*?" HE looked around, having not realized he was the only one without a means of self-defense. He quickly searched and found a large branch on the ground, as big as a small rifle. "There, this will do." Avonaco sighed, taking a dagger from his belt and some leather, and tossing it to Sebastian. "Tie that to it and you'll have a better chance my friend."

Avonaco returned his focus to the group, continuing to prepare them. "Now, you must stab strike its heart. Just grazing it will not kill it, so you need to strike it in the heart as fast as possible." Everyone nodded, cocking guns and readying spears. He then said a few words in Algonquian, then the group began moving towards the cave. Ashleigh tightened her grip on the dagger, looking to see Sebastian tighten the last knot on his makeshift weapon. As they neared the entrance, Ashleigh watched the sky get darker, the sun setting lower and lower. Sebastian saw her face get pale, and he rested his hand on her shoulder. She jumped at first, but she relaxed when she saw it was only him. "We'll get her back. I promise." She smiled, thankful that though it all he was always by her side every step of the way. She refocused herself, and walked headfirst into the Wendigo den.

When they entered the cave, she was met with a foul odor. It reminded her of when Eren would find dead rats hidden in walls of the bar, only this was much fouler, with a metallic smell rather than the usual rat smell. She looked at the ground and saw the blood trail darken, bits of meat strewn across the floor. The further they went the thicker the smell became. It felt like the entire cave was some abandoned meat cellar, left to whoever found it first. "How will we know what it looks like when we see it?" Ashleigh asked. Sebastian studied the cave, trying his best to watch for unexpected attacks. "Well, most the descriptions I've heard of involve either a shaggy appearance, yellow skin, or even if it's over 10 feet tall." Ashleigh's eyes widened, her grip tightening on the blade. "Well that's... quite a variety..." "He nodded, watching as the others went further in. "Yes, but one common trait that most the descriptions share is that the creatures have large yellow teeth and antlers. Not sure why, but they do." She looked around the cave, watching for anything that might stick out. For a moment, nothing seemed too strange, until she saw the light.

At the end of the cave was a dim light, leaving flickering shadows on the ground. Avonaco halted the group, motioning for Ashleigh and Sebastian to come forward. "I think its best if Ashleigh stays behind while we go ahead first. Sebastian, I want you to-" He was cut off by Ashleigh stepping past them. "I swear to God if one more person tries telling me to sit on the sidelines then that Wendigo won't be the only one getting it's ass kicked." Before she got any further, Sebastian grabbed her arm; she looked back at him, seeing he was almost angry in a way. "Look I understand you have a lot of emotions right now, but we can't just rush in there. Neither of us have dealt with something like this before and we need to think this through..."

"Let me tell you what I've been thinking about Sebastian," she stated. "I've thought about why you don't tell me things, I've thought about how I've felt like a lost dog following the first person to show any interest in it, and I've thought about how I've had it with people telling me that they think I should do this or that." She wretched her arm away from Sebastian, turning to face him directly. "I know you do the things you do cause you worry about what I might think of you after. But maybe consider that I want to know these things because it will make us closer and help me understand. That way I don't have to feel like I need to ask every person who knows you to explain why you act the way you do. Now do please tell me, what I haven't thought about because I am sick and tired of thinking you see me as a simple child who can't handle knowing details about who you are."

She then walked off towards the light, readying her dagger. She was sick of it all and decided to take things into her own hands. As she neared it, the rotten smell got worse and worse. And with that smell came a faint noise... a child's whimper. She rushed ahead, her thoughts clouded and her heart racing. When she entered the room, she was met with a small fire on the ground, a chunk of meat roasting above it. She looked around the room and saw old bones and rotten meat. And next to the fire, was Sybil in a makeshift basket. She went to towards her, until she heard a low groan.

She turned to see a matted mound of fur and peaking from the fur were two antlers. She watched as it made slow breathing motions. She quickly backed away, turning around to see Sebastian and Avonaco standing at the entrance of the room. Their eyes were wide with panic, Avonaco lifting his rifle. "Ashleigh," Sebastian whispered. "Slowly walk towards us. When your out of the way we'll take the shot." She began to step towards them, trying to be as silent as possible. As she moved, the creature adjusted itself, stretching one of its arms. She could see its hand had sharp claws and was stained red and brown. But what stuck to her wasn't the claws or color, but that the hand itself was no bigger than her own. The creature pulled its hand back and curled itself up in a ball. She turned back to see Sybil. For a moment, she thought she might be able to silently retrieve her, but she could see that Sebastian was waiting for her to come forward. Part of her wanted to listen to him, to trust that he knew what he was doing. But something else was shouting over that side of herself. And she couldn't ignore it.

She turned on her heels and rushed for Sybil. On the way she kicked a bone across the floor, the sound echoing across the stone floor. Without hesitation. The creature jumped up and rushed Ashleigh, knocking her to the side. She was thrown into the wall, her body feeling like a horse had kicked her with full force. Suddenly, a shot rang out in the cave, and the creature let out a painful wail. It thrust its hands into the pile of bones and threw them towards the entryway, causing Sebastian and Avonaco to back away. It turned back towards Ashleigh and she could see the creature in full view.

She was, in many ways, a wild animal. Her hair was matted, the horns protruding though her forehead with other small horns. She had what looked like bear skin just covering her upper half, with torn up clothing covering her lower half; her claws black and her teeth were yellow, with markings and scars covering most her body. But her eyes looked like an inferno, black pupils centered in savage flames. Ashleigh tried to stand up, but the creature tried to swipe her claws at her midriff. She was able to back away, but not unscathed. She could feel blood soaking her clothes, nothing serious, but it was there, she looked back at the entrance and saw Sebastian came into view, his eyes wide in panic. He went to say something but was cut off by the creature letting lose a powerful howl. It sounds like a mix between a wolf and a screaming child, piercing even the strongest of ears.

The creature got low to the ground, looking ready to pounce. Ashleigh looked back to Sybil, her small body moving back and forth in the small basket. She wanted nothing more to keep her safe, but she ended up putting her in the worst possible situation. All she could do, was try her best to keep her safe. She then turned back tom face the Wendigo, lifting her dagger up and making eye contact with the creature. All she could see in its eyes her hate, hunger, and something else... something twisted. It screamed one more time, and then leaped at Ashleigh. She lifted the blade, aiming for its heart and hoping she could land the hit. The creature knocked her down to the ground, causing them both to roll across he cave floor and into the fire. They finally crashed against the wall, the creature laying on top of Ashleigh. Sebastian rushed inside, moving the creature's body out of the way, he then saw that Ashleigh had in fact landed the killing blow with the dagger. "Ashleigh wake up. Are you alright?" He then saw the cuts across her stomach left by the Wendigo. He quickly took off his coat and pressed it against her stomach, to which she quickly punched him in the face.

"For the love of-!" he said holding his nose. "What in God's name was that for?" "You pressed against the cuts in my stomach and I reacted to the pain," she said. "Which, by the way, never do that again please…" She rubbed her stomach and slowly stood up. "If we're talking about what not to do again, perhaps you should add 'running into the den of a cannibalistic monster' then?" he remarked. She quickly rushed to pick up Sybil, "Honestly what were you thinking when you did that? You could have died, and I don't want that on my conscience. I already have enough on it as is…" Ashleigh sighed, checking to make sure Sybil had no cuts or wounds. "I know, I know. I just had a lot on my mind and the emotions all mixed together and- "She turned to see that his expression changed, a look of shock and anger replacing his concern for her. "What do you mean you know? How do you know if I haven't told you…" he stopped for a moment and rolled his eye's. "Of course, he told you he always does things like that." He began pacing the room, his hands rubbing his head. "This isn't how I wanted it this was not supposed to be how it happened. I suppose you think of me as some monster with what I was connected to? Or perhaps you think me of a fool because I can't seem to leave the church behind fully. Go on say it all why don't you? Treat me like something that you can't stand to look at-"

She slapped him mid-sentence, tears welling up in her eyes. "Don't ever presume to think you know how I see you. I admire you and would go to the ends of the earth for you. I trust you with my life and then some. If you really think I'm going to see you any different than I did before then you're damn fool." He stood there silent, nothing to say with only a blank expression, the only sound being the crackling flames and sybils breathing "I was so set in the idea that you just didn't trust me like you did everyone else, thinking that I couldn't handle anything you would have told me. But I understand that you were scared, and you feared what I might've thought of you. I won't think anything different of you and you should know that."

She placed her hand on his shoulder. "I'm sorry I found out the dishonest way. I just wanted to understand you. And in doing so I overstepped a boundary you set and in understand if you want to part ways..." "Alice," he replied. She was caught of guard by the sudden response. "I'm sorry?" she asked. "My mother. Her name was Alice. And my sibling's names were Jacob and Edith. They were only 11 when they passed that day." Ashleigh didn't know how to respond. "The only person who knows that is Johnathan, and even then, he doesn't always understand my anger." He reached for her hand, holding it in between his own. "You are the first person I've met in a long time that I want to have around. Shaman has his own life here and Clyde just takes me places. But you, you actually want to travel with me. And to be quite frank, I am terrified. I'm terrified I'm going to lose someone who gives more than a damn about me."

They stood in silence for a moment, unsure of how to respond to one another. That is, until Avonaco entered the room. "I hate to finally interrupt your moment," he said. "But we do need to finish killing the Wendigo Miskwà Inini. There is more to do after stabbing its heart." He walked to the corpse, followed by the other two men, one carrying a larger blade then the others. Avonaco took the silver blade from the creature's heart, handing it to Ashleigh. She took it, staring at the black liquid that stained the blade and seeing just how little human the woman was. "We must ensure the creature stays dead, otherwise it may come back for more blood." Ashleigh looked at him concerned. "How do you plan on doing that?" she asked. He turned back to face the corpse, watching one of the men lay her out in the shape of an X, with the other readying his blade. "We separate her into pieces," he said. "Then we cut out the heart and bury it in a box. And for good measure, we burn the rest, leaving the ash for the wind." With that last word, the man swung his blade down, a heavy thwack echoing in the cave.

Later when they returned, they were greeted by the chief and a worried Neha. She looked relieved to see Sybil was unharmed, continuing to apologize for her failure, to which Ashleigh assured her she was not to blame. Avonaco told the chief of Ashleigh's reckless acts, rushing in to save the child and single handedly killing a Wendigo on her own. When she returned the blade to the chief he looked to Ashleigh and gave her a silent nod, to which later Shaman would explain that he respected her for keeping to her word. During all the commotion she had forgotten that she had said she would kill the monster herself.

They continued with the previously planned festivities, adding in the defeat of the monster. Everyone around her was celebrating, some dancing and others sitting around a fire and speaking happily to one another. All except Ashleigh, who just couldn't seem to get in the spirits. She watched from a distance as Sebastian happily spoke with Shaman and other Cheyenne, making them laugh the entire time. After a few moments, the chief came to sit next to her, holding a large pipe; he took a rather large puff, breathing heavy smelling smoke in the air. He then offered it to Ashleigh who, kindly turned it away. She had tried smoking pipes before with Eren and the Major in her youth, and she could never handle the smoke that came from it.

The chief set the pipe down, reaching for the silver blade he had given her prior. The blood had been cleaned off, though a black tint was still visible. "Would you like to know the importance of this blade?" he asked her. She turned to him and silently nodded. He looked down at the blade, the fire causing his reflection to flicker. "When I was a boy, my father before me told me stories of the Wendigo, of how it could sometimes look like a man but easily change. One day, we met a very interesting man. He was of your people, skin pale like snow and hair black as coal; he wished to trade pelts with my father, hoping for something valuable. The entire time they spoke, I hid behind my father, worried this man was a Wendigo. When he finally asked about my unwarranted fear, my father told him of our beliefs in the creature. He looked down at me and smiled, telling my father he had he wanted to give me something to make me feel better. My father told me to present myself, and so I did. The man then pulled out a pure silver blade, he presented it to me, telling me that if I were to ever encounter a Wendigo, I would have this blade to protect me.

"He died later that year, killed by another tribe outside our own. My father found him, no scalp and left to the animals. He was kind to give him a proper funeral as you would say, out of respect for the kindness he showed us." Ashleigh wasn't sure how to respond. "Why give this to me if it's that important?" she asked. The chief looked at her and smiled, with nothing but kindness visible from his expression. "He saw something in me worth giving me this blade. And today I think I saw that in you." He handed her the blade, to which she took it slowly. "You'll need it if you plan on keeping the Miskwà Inini alive from here on." She looked down at the blade, and then back to Sebastian. "I don't know if I can," she said. The chief picked up the pipe and took another long puff, breathing a large plume of smoke. "We are not always sure of what we can or cannot do. That is why we do the things we do, to learn from the things we can't do, and keep doing the things we can." He stood up, kicking the log that Ashleigh sat on. "Go. Sit with him," he said. "You should be celebrating with him." He then walked off, leaving her to her own devices. She looked back down at the blade, thinking of what he said. We do the things we do, so that we learn from what we can't do, and keep doing the things we can. she then laughed to herself, thinking of all the things she knew she would have to do soon.

She stood up and walked over to Sebastian and his crowd. She politely asked one of the Cheyenne next to him to make room taking a seat at his side. "So," she asked. "What stories have you been telling that they enjoy so much? I think I'd love to hear them." Sebastian looked between them, afraid to answer. "I don't think you'll like them, they're boring. We could talk about something else-" She lifted her finger and cut him off. "Sebastian it doesn't matter if I like it or if I don't. What matters is that its coming from you. I want to hear you tell the stories." It was short, but Sebastian enjoyed how she wanted to hear more about his past, even knowing what she did. Shaman looked at her from behind Sebastian and nodded his head, assuring Ashleigh that things would be fine from here on.

"Now go on, tell us more. What is it that was so entertaining to them?" Sebastian looked between the onlookers, and back to Ashleigh, thinking to himself of how lucky he was to have found her. "Well," he began. "I was just telling them of how I got my name, Miskwà Inini. As exciting as you might think it may be, its actually rather embarrassing." "Well coming from you, that doesn't surprise me." He laughed at the remark, to which the others around them stared. Shaman quickly repeated the conversation and, when finished, the crowd laughed in turn. From there Sebastian continued to tell his stories, bringing a much-needed light to the occasion.

Once the festivities ended, everyone prepared to rest for the night. With everything that had transpired, Ashleigh was ready for a well needed rest. Sebastian had just finished setting up their tipi with Shamans help, Ashleigh having prepared Sybil for rest. She remained quiet, unphased by most anything that had happened earlier in the day. "She can't stay with us," Sebastian said. She turned to him and saw the look he was giving her. "With what we do it's too dangerous for her to stay around us. We need to find her a proper home." Ashleigh looked back to Sybil, not wanting to admit that Sebastian was right. The truth of the matter was that she really couldn't stay with them. Wherever they went there would be danger, and with that danger came the risk of potential death. Not to mention that neither of them had and proper experience raising a child.

"I can find her a home," Shaman said. The two looked at him surprised by his answer. "You can?" Ashleigh asked. "Yes. I understand that its common practice to leave a newborn at the steps of a church, to which the people there will care for the child. Perhaps you can take her there? There's a settlement not far from here that we could take her to." Sebastian looked between the two of them, pondering the idea. "That isn't a bad idea," he said. "Although it depends on what you want to do Ashleigh." Ashleigh looked over the child, watching the way she breathed in her small basket. "You've met these people before Shaman?" she asked. "Yes, I've met them. This is also the settlement where I do most of my trading for the tribe." She looked between him and Sybil, thinking that there was only one possible course of action to take.

"We can take her there in the morning," she said. "How much more time do you need here Sebastian?" He looked in his shoulder bag, checking on the medicine Shaman had made him. "I have enough medicine for now, so we should be fine to take her and leave by the afternoon. Shaman, you wouldn't happen to know where we could go next after we find a place to take Sybil do you?" he asked, Shaman stroked his beard, contemplating the thought for a moment. "Actually," he responded. "There is, in fact, somewhere that I think you two would be most needed. Somewhere Southeast. I've heard tales of specious things happening somewhere and you may be interested." Sebastian looked to Ashleigh, waiting for a sign of approval. "Well?" he asked. "What say you?" Ashleigh look out past the plains and the night sky, wondering what may lay around the corner. "What the hell," she said. We've come this far. Why not see what else there is for us to encounter?"

About The Author

"Meet Mike and Jon, a father and son duo with a passion for writing. The son from a small town in Wyoming and the father from a small town in New York; one with a passion for history and learning about other cultures. The other loves the supernatural, legends and lore, and other oddities."

Printed in the United States
By Bookmasters